y X   2165810
Roth, David
The girl in the grass

y
Roth, David   2165810
The girl in the grass

So novel

The Girl
in the Grass

DAVID ROTH

THE GIRL

IN

THE GRASS

a novel

BEAUFORT BOOKS, INC.

New York / Toronto

No character in this book is intended to
represent any actual person; all the incidents of the
story are entirely fictional in nature.

Library of Congress Cataloging in Publication Data

Roth, David.
The girl in the grass.

Summary: Seventeen-year-old Tom Stevens sets out to
locate a sister whose existence had been unknown to him.
[1. Brothers and sisters—Fiction]
I. Title.
PZ7.R7275Gi   [Fic]   81-18091
ISBN 0-8253-0086-X   AACR2

Published in the United States by Beaufort Books, Inc.,
New York. Published simultaneously in Canada by
General Publishing Co. Limited

Designer: Ellen LoGiudice

Printed in the U.S.A.   First Edition
10 9 8 7 6 5 4 3 2 1

For CILLA, *my best hope for all things both beautiful and good.*

Note:

The alert reader may decide that the city of Boston in this book is Boston, Massachusetts. He or she will be wrong, for Boston has been reinvented here especially for the occasion, as also is the case with Cape Ann. There is no Shepherd Island on any map of the area, nor can it possibly be a familiar landmark to the local residents.

Part 1

THE GIRL WITH LONG, GOLDEN HAIR

Chapter One

ALONE IN HIS ROOM, whenever he felt sure he would not be disturbed, Tom wrote down these thoughts:

1. The girl with long, golden hair.
2. The field by the sea—the grass, the wind, the gulls circling.
3. The girl is singing.

He wrote these same thoughts a dozen, a hundred different ways, changing their order, slipping new words in and out. He wrote them slowly, wrote them quickly; he wrote them with his eyes closed, with his eyes open. The closest he came to understanding them was when he heard a fleeting piece of melody: this was the girl's song. The melody left his head as quickly as it came, but still, these were the best times.

The worst times were when his eyes would blur with tears and he wouldn't know why, except he was filled with a terrible sense of loss.

Sometimes he was afraid he might be crazy, to have thoughts like these, that came out of nowhere, again and again, never leaving him alone for long. But he also knew that he was seventeen and well liked at school by most of the other kids and did well at his studies, particularly English and science, and liked girls, although he was shy with them; and this did not seem to him to be the profile of someone who was crazy.

But just the same, he did not share these thoughts with anyone, not Uncle Carl or Aunt Belle, not with any of his friends at school, not even Wayne. Just in case he was crazy, he thought it best to hide it from everyone else.

The little fragment of song, the girl with long, golden hair . . . and shadows he couldn't name, somehow more terrible than all the rest.

In the early part of July the first real heat of summer came. Many of the houses in Delmory sprouted air conditioners; window shades were down all day in the row apartments on Poole Street, and in the residential district of Willow Hill drapes were pulled closed against the noontime sun. In July Delmory slipped a thousand miles south, into Georgia, and everyone imagined it was as hot as it could be.

Despite the heat wave, Uncle Carl felt that they should go ahead with their plans to spend a long weekend in Boston. Of course, Tom agreed. Aunt Belle was outnumbered from the start.

"It's too hot," she said.

"Boston has a sea breeze," Uncle Carl replied.

"And everything is air-conditioned," Tom added.

"What about the mobs of tourists?"

"We'll beat away the crowds," Uncle Carl said. He winked at Tom. "Promise you, Belle, we'll protect you."

"I'll stay right behind you and Uncle Carl can walk in front. No one will dare bump into you."

Aunt Belle made a face at them. "You two are always ganging up on me. What chance do I have?"

Uncle Carl burst into laughter. His round face grew red as he brought out a handkerchief to wipe sweat off his forehead. He was too heavy to be comfortable in summer, yet he always said it was his favorite time of year.

"Listen to her, Tom. Now she's the poor, helpless heroine and we're the meanies."

Aunt Belle pretended to be insulted. By now it was a game. "Don't you laugh at me, Carl Stevens!"

Tom nodded. "Maybe we should go without her, Uncle Carl. We'll have more fun that way."

Aunt Belle reached over the table to swat Tom with her half of the evening newspaper. She missed as he jumped up from his chair. She chased him into the living room. As small as Uncle Carl was big, she moved with nervous quickness. She caught him before he could reach the front door.

"Are you going to stop plaguing an old woman?" she demanded.

Tom nodded and she released him.

"Do you really want to go to Boston."

"Yes."

She sighed. Uncle Carl was in the doorway sipping his coffee, watching them. His huge frame nearly filled the opening.

"And you, you big lug, I suppose you're bound to go?"

"Three days, Belle. We'll drive there Friday morning,

come home Sunday afternoon. I've already made reservations at the Parkway Hotel. You know how much you like the Parkway."

"That's true," Aunt Belle said. "They do have such an elegant dining room."

"Then we can go?" Tom asked.

She ruffled his hair. "You knew I'd give in all along."

Tom kissed her and ran out the door into the summer evening.

Tom's part-time summer job was at Olson's Drugstore downtown, stocking shelves and cleaning floors. He reached the store by ten after six, only a few minutes late. Mr. Olson looked at the clock as he came in.

Tom was a hard worker. He had a short, muscular, compact body that was capable of carrying boxes in piles ten high. His dark hair, his deep tan from afternoons at the lake, his ruddy, healthy complexion all combined to make him look older than seventeen. His hands were too large for the rest of him, but they were skillful, not clumsy, as he emptied cartons of shampoo, toothpaste and shaving cream onto the store's shelves.

Mr. Olson watched him awhile, then grunted and went back to the pharmacy counter. Tom found him there later and asked him if he could have off Friday.

"Friday?" Mr. Olson continued to bottle a prescription. "That's a busy night."

"I know, but we're going to Boston and . . ."

"The big city, eh?" Mr. Olson began typing a label for the bottle. The snap of the keys punctuated his words. "I haven't been to Boston in years. I'm stuck in this store seven days a week."

Tom looked away, at the mountain of cartons that still had to be unpacked before closing time.

Mr. Olson cleared his throat. "Tell you what, Tom. If you can get that skinny friend of yours . . ."

"Wayne?"

"Yeah, the one who's always hanging around here anyway, waiting till you get done, drooling over at the soda fountain."

"That's Wayne."

Mr. Olson pushed his glasses back up his nose. "Get him to come in for you and you can have Friday off."

"Great. I'll ask him tonight." Tom started back toward his boxes. "Thank you, Mr. Olson."

"One more thing, son."

Tom stopped.

"If you came in early once in a while, it would make up for when you're late."

"Okay, Mr. Olson."

"That's all."

Tom walked up the aisle between the tobacco and the candy. Behind him Mr. Olson began to whistle through his teeth.

Wayne came by for him before ten. Tom worked until a few minutes after the hour because he'd come in late, then said good night to Mr. Olson and hurried out with his friend at his side. Together they walked through downtown Delmory. Only Star's Pizza and the movie theater were still open. Near the VFW park, people were sitting out on their front steps. Cigarettes glowed in the dark. A cool breeze came from the park, rustling through the trees.

"Nice night," Wayne said. He nudged Tom and pointed toward two girls walking ahead of them.

"Yeah, I see them," Tom said. He was tired from the intense pace of his work at the drugstore. Sweat dried on his face as they walked.

Wayne, who was taller and much thinner than Tom, quickened his steps. Tom hurried to keep up. They followed the girls into the park.

"Where'd they go?" Wayne complained when they realized the two girls had disappeared.

"Beats me," Tom said.

"Let's circle around, see if we can intercept them." Wayne started off to his left. "Got a line ready?"

"What?"

"Got a line ready?"

Tom shook his head. "No, I haven't got a line ready. Do you?"

"How about, 'Good evening, ladies. Do you know that some of the boats down on the pond aren't locked up at night?' "

Tom laughed.

"Well, think of something better."

Tom was silent.

"Don't you want to try to pick them up?"

"Maybe." Tom looked around at the black shapes of the trees. Something was in flower, filling the air with a rich perfume. "Fact is, we didn't get a good look at them."

"So? Do you have a more pressing engagement with a guaranteed beauty?"

"Nope."

Wayne sighed. "Sometimes I think we're socially retarded."

They followed the path into the bandstand area above the pond. There was no sign of the two girls.

"Damn," Wayne said. "I felt lucky tonight, too."

"Let's sit down. My feet are killing me."

They slumped onto a bench and stared up at the trees above the bandstand. Tom could smell the water plants that grew and rotted around the edge of the pond. The night was lush, overripe from the heat.

"Want to work for me this Friday?" he asked.

"For old man Olson?"

"Yeah."

"Where are you going?"

"Boston with my aunt and uncle."

"I don't know. He's such a grouch."

"Come on. I'll give you my pay for Friday. The whole amount, not just what's left after taxes."

"I don't think he likes me."

"Fact is, he admires you."

"What do you mean?"

Tom hid a grin by turning away. "Just tonight he was telling me how lucky I am to have a friend loyal enough to come by to meet me every night. He was thinking about breaking you in on the soda fountain."

"Yeah?"

"Would I lie to you?"

"Sure, if you thought that was the only way you could get me to work for you."

Tom shook his head. "I don't believe you said that."

"Do you really need me to work for you?"

"I'd appreciate it."

"Yeah, I guess. But he'd better not breathe down my neck all night the way he does you."

"He's okay." Tom saw a movement at the far side of the bandstand. "Here come those girls."

Wayne quickly got to his feet. Tom pulled him back. "Give them a chance, will you? They're coming this way, if you don't scare them off."

He and Wayne stared out toward the pond, keeping track of the girls' approach from the corners of their eyes.

Tom could hear them giggling over something one was telling the other. Wayne was twitching beside him.

"Go, tiger," Tom whispered as the girls crossed the path in front of them.

Wayne cleared his throat. "Nice night, isn't it?" he asked the girls.

They turned but didn't break stride.

"Nicer on the pond," Wayne continued. "And I happen to know for a fact that . . ."

"Buzz off, creep!" the girl closest to them said.

"Hey, come on," Wayne persisted valiantly. "We're just two lonely guys who would love to take you rowing on the duck pond."

"Take a couple of ducks," the second girl said.

Tom listened to their laughter as they hurried away. "I think you need to refine your approach a little."

Wayne slumped back on the bench. "A lot of help you were."

Tom shrugged. "I didn't like mine anyway."

"How the hell did you know which was going to be yours?" Wayne demanded. Then he realized Tom was joking and punched him in the ribs. "Socially retarded," he muttered. "For sure."

They walked slowly back toward Willow Hill. It was after eleven. The porches were nearly empty now.

"I was going to concentrate my main efforts on Cheryl Babcock this summer," Wayne told him. "You know, that little cheerleader who's always bubbling all over the place."

"Yeah, I know the one. So why aren't you?"

Wayne doubled up his fists and feinted at the air. "Her folks had to go rent a house for the summer on Shepherd Island off Cape Ann. They're . . ."

16

Tom stiffened. "There aren't any houses on Shepherd Island."

"Says who?"

"I . . . I don't know." Tom tried to hide his confusion by walking faster.

"Then why do you say there aren't any?"

Something was flashing through Tom's mind: shattered images, like a slide show gone crazy. There was a strange metallic taste in his mouth.

"What's wrong, Tom?"

"I just had a flash about Shepherd Island, the second I heard you say it." Tom forced himself to walk more slowly. "It's nothing."

"What do you mean, a flash?"

"Like I know it."

Wayne glanced at him several times as they walked on. Tom tried to laugh.

"I guess someone must have told me there are no houses on Shepherd Island. Or I read it somewhere. Somehow it stuck in my head. But hell, it's probably all developed by now."

"Maybe I could hitch up there," Wayne said. "Trouble is, Cheryl Babcock doesn't even know I'm alive."

Tom's street cut off to the right. He said good night to Wayne.

"Yeah, see you tomorrow," Wayne called. In a moment he was gone, leaping into the shadows.

Tom walked two blocks down his street, then climbed the steps onto his front porch. The living room windows glowed with the flickering light from the television. He sat on the porch railing, but he was somewhere else, seeing the field by the sea again, the tall brown grass bending in the sea wind. There were voices, laughter, then for a moment

17

an image of the girl with long, golden hair, her face hidden behind her hair, the wind blowing over her. And she was humming the song, her song. . . .

"Tom, are you out there?"

He stood up straight, a feeling like guilt coming over him at being caught with these thoughts. But it wasn't guilt, it was . . .

"Come in, Tom," Aunt Belle was shouting. "Get some of this watermelon before your uncle pigs it all." There was the sound of a scuffle inside. Aunt Belle laughed. "And regrets it tomorrow."

"Okay," Tom called. "I'll be right in."

The night was silent and now the sea and the grass were gone; the song also fading back into its hiding place. He blinked back tears and wondered where they came from.

He had almost betrayed himself when Wayne mentioned Shepherd Island. . . .

He had never been to Cape Ann in his life. Why did he feel so sure there were no houses of any kind on Shepherd Island?

"Is something wrong?" Aunt Belle called.

"No. I'm coming."

He went inside, closing the screen door behind him very gently, as if any loud noise might bring his world tumbling down around him.

Chapter Two

SUMMER IN BOSTON, the streets painted in heat waves, the colors all seeming to blur together as they drove toward the Parkway Hotel. Tom sat in front beside Uncle Carl, Aunt Belle preferring the relative safety of the back seat, where she sat buckled into her seat belt, periodically covering her eyes with her hands as Uncle Carl expertly shifted lanes.

"How can people live like this every day?" Aunt Belle wondered out loud, a note of panic edging into her voice.

Uncle Carl laughed. "I expect many of them even enjoy it."

There were splashes of green as they passed Boston Common and signs for an outdoor art show. People on their lunch break wandered by exhibits of paintings and sculpture. Tom got Aunt Belle's attention.

"We'll have to go over to see it," he said.

"Right now I'll settle for my room at the Parkway."

"Now Belle, you know damn well you get a thrill out of all this." Uncle Carl swerved to avoid a taxi, then squeezed right to make a turn onto a side street. "You just don't want to let on you're having fun."

Horns blared. Traffic slid to a halt behind a street repair crew. Jackhammers split the noon heat into sharp slivers. Aunt Belle took her hands off her eyes and put them over her ears.

The Parkway Hotel rose in faded splendor uptown at the edge of an area of urban decay. In sight of the hotel's high curved windows, whole blocks of derelict apartment houses huddled around the burned out shells left by busy arsonists. But in the hotel itself an air of past elegance was tenaciously clung to: the high chandeliers still burned, the red velvet upholstery on the lobby furniture had recently been cleaned, the room rates were still outrageous. As Tom rode up in one of the elevators with his aunt and uncle, he felt the great steel box creak around them, as if it were tired from its long years of service, but still strong, still capable, still more than happy to carry yet one more party of guests up to their rooms.

Tom had a small room adjoining the larger one the desk had assigned his aunt and uncle. From its one window he could see the green belt along the river, dozens of sailboats on the blue water, like clusters of bright butterflies.

His uncle leaned into his room. "I'm going over to Cambridge to find out why I haven't received that shipment of stoves yet," he said. Uncle Carl owned a large appliance store in Delmory. He smiled now. "Got to tend to business first."

"Can I come?"

"I imagine your aunt would like to do a little shopping. I'd appreciate your going with her."

Tom nodded, hiding his disappointment. Aunt Belle was already in the bathroom, changing into another outfit, humming to herself.

Uncle Carl winked. "She's the biggest dear phony I've ever known." He picked up his briefcase, which seemed dwarfed in his large hands, and strode to the door. "Mind you take good care of her."

"I will."

"I know you will." He disappeared into the corridor and a moment later Tom heard the elevator creaking as it came for him.

"I'll be ready in just a minute," Aunt Belle called from the bathroom.

"No hurry." Tom walked to a window and looked out again. The streets below crisscrossed away from the hotel, leading in all directions at once. For a moment the possibilities staggered him. He felt as if he'd been living in a cocoon all these years in Delmory, away from life, protected. Now, here, on this Boston summer's day, he felt the cocoon begin to crack.

Tom spent the afternoon with Aunt Belle shopping the giant stores downtown. They clawed their way through the crowds in the bargain basement under Filene's before seeking refuge in the airy, more refined upper levels, then went on to Jordan Marsh. Tom hid his boredom and remained attentive to his aunt. She bribed him with a late lunch of sticky desserts, then launched her attack on the little shops on Newbury Street. By the time they headed back toward the hotel, the sun was a brassy furnace in the west and Tom could not keep up with her under the weight of all her bundles.

"Don't drop that box," she cautioned as they entered the cool shadows of the Parkway's lobby.

"Which one?" Tom muttered. He bumped into an over-stuffed chair and took a new fix on the bank of elevators at the far side of the lobby.

"Careful!"

Tom stopped, sensed someone stepping around him, then started again toward the elevators.

"Tom, for heaven's sake, can't you even see where you're going?"

"Nope."

Aunt Belle removed a parcel that had been riding against his nose. "Does that help?"

Tom grunted.

"Well then, come along. If I'd known you were going to be so much trouble, I would have gone alone."

Tom grunted again.

"What's that?"

The elevator door slid shut. "Nothing."

"If your Uncle Carl isn't back, we'll just take a minute and duck out to that cute little boutique we passed on the corner. I . . ."

Tom groaned and shifted his load. His left arm had lost all feeling.

"Very well!" his aunt said. "You've made your point.'"

Uncle Carl met them at the door and helped Tom unload. "For God's sake, Tom," he said, "how could you be so selfish?"

Tom looked at him.

"Didn't you let your poor aunt buy anything for herself?"

Aunt Belle slapped at him with her purse. "I asked him if

he wanted anything. They had some lovely dress shirts down at Filene's. He would have looked so nice in one of them."

Tom rolled his eyes. His uncle laughed.

"Go ahead, you two. Always ganging up on me. I suppose you approve of the way he goes around in those ratty blue jeans all the time." She pushed one of the parcels into Uncle Carl's hands. "Here, this is for you, not that you deserve it."

Tom headed toward his room.

"Tom, make sure you dress for dinner," Aunt Belle called after him. "We're eating in the dining room downstairs and you're not going in those jeans."

"Okay," Tom said.

"Go ahead, open it," Aunt Belle was telling Uncle Carl. "It's just the thing for you to wear when you're playing golf."

On Saturday they toured Faneuil Hall and Quincy Markets, visited the Aquarium, and ate a big lunch in a restaurant on the waterfront. That night they went to the movies. Tom didn't get off by himself until Sunday morning when he woke up early and slipped out before his aunt and uncle stirred.

It had rained during the night and the streets were still wet. A brisk wind was blowing the clouds away.

Tom wandered through the streets for hours, keeping track of the time by clocks that he passed. Checkout time at the hotel was at noon and he had to be back before then. But he stretched out his free time as long as he could, wondering what it would be like to be on his own, living in a city like Boston.

He treated himself to a cup of coffee and a roll at a table

outside a café, wandered in and out of a couple of book-stores. Almost all the other shops were closed this early on Sunday. He bought a paperback novel in one store and jammed it into his back pocket as he walked on. He followed two girls around Beacon Hill, almost spoke to one sitting on a bench in the Public Gardens.

It was getting late when he crossed onto the Common, but he had suddenly remembered the art show there and wanted to take a quick look. Many of the exhibits were just opening, the paintings being hung again on the makeshift canvas backdrops. People wandered through the area, Sunday newspapers under their arms, stopping before paintings that caught their attention.

Tom strolled with the crowd, as intrigued by the people as by the paintings. Most of the work was abstract and didn't interest him. Then, before a group of three land-scapes, he stopped short, so riveted by what he saw that he didn't feel people bumping into him.

For he was looking at the field by the sea that had haunted him all his life.

Not paintings of any field or any sea, but his field, his sea. The grass, brown as if it had never tasted rain, was bending to a wind that he could feel, for it was his wind.

He was afraid he was going to be sick. He blinked sweat out of his eyes, but when his sight cleared again, there were the paintings, as if someone had looked inside his head and painted *his* thoughts.

One painting showed the empty field against a faded blue sea, under a sky of high, white clouds. In the second, a young girl with long hair sat playing a guitar in a nest of grass sheltered from the sea wind. Sunlight swept across the painting from the right, catching gold highlights in the brown grass, in the girl's long hair. Her face was deathly

24

white, not innocent as a child's face should be, and yet she was young, no more than twelve or thirteen.

Tom stepped closer, a raw, metallic taste burning his mouth. There was another figure in this painting, almost hidden in the grass nest, a small boy sitting near the girl, maybe two or three years old, neatly camouflaged by the wisps of grass that covered him. He was playing with a wooden toy, a carved animal. . . .

Tom was running away before he realized he had started, his legs pumping with a will all their own. He ducked through the crowd until he found shelter behind some wooden sheds, where he lost the coffee and roll he had eaten earlier. Gradually, the trembling left his legs, and he leaned against the wall of one shed, trying to sort out what had happened. . . .

He knew he had to go back. He had to find out the name of the artist, and then too, there was the third painting, the one he had not looked at closely yet.

He started toward the art exhibit. His feet didn't want to go there. It was all like a dream, happening in broad daylight on Boston Common, a bad dream that at any moment he should wake up from. Only if there was a way to wake up from this dream, he couldn't find it.

Chapter Three

THE THIRD PAINTING waited there for him, beside the others. It was as if he were alone on the Common, walking through a tunnel, he on one end, that painting on the other. And then he was there.

In the third painting the sea was invisible, and yet he sensed that it was not far away. Instead of the wild field, there was a yard of the same brown grass, cluttered with rabbit hutches, tires, an abandoned automobile. But what filled most of the picture was the house, a rambling series of tacked on additions, and a flag, too large, too bright, that flew over it all, rippling in the sea wind, which blew here too, out of sight of the sea.

Tom swallowed his rising panic and moved closer. Again the girl was playing her guitar, this time from her perch on top of a rabbit hutch. The little boy played with his toy wooden animal in the grass at her feet.

Tom looked at the house. The figure of a man filled one window; he was a blur behind white curtains. The wind blew even here, in his room, tugging at the fabric of the curtains as if to blow them to one side.

He could not stay; he could not bear to look upon these paintings for another moment. He found a short notice pinned to the backdrop:

> SYLVIA MACY has been painting in oils since her teens. More recently she has begun working with acrylic polymer mediums. She has exhibited in several Boston galleries. The three paintings hung here are on loan from private collections and not for sale. Ms. Macy is noted for the dramatic content of her work as well as for her technical virtuosity.

He read it twice. It told him nothing, except her name. Glancing quickly back at the paintings, he saw the same swirled signature in the lower right corner of each canvas: Sylvia Macy, who somehow had the same pictures in her head that he had in his . . .

People moving by him broke his reverie. He remembered his aunt and uncle at the hotel. It must be late; he had to get back.

He walked from the Common into the Public Gardens. All his life as far back as he could remember, he had had these thoughts, these pictures of the field by the sea and the girl with long, golden hair. Now, suddenly, they had been

27

wrenched violently out of the privacy of his mind and put on public exhibition by someone who shared them intimately.

Who was Sylvia Macy? Why did she share his visions? And what, underneath it all, did these visions mean?

Uncle Carl and Aunt Belle were waiting for him in the hotel lobby. The suitcases and bags and boxes containing Aunt Belle's purchases made a small mountain between them. Uncle Carl's neck was red. It was twelve-thirty.

As soon as Aunt Belle saw him coming through the front doors, she rushed over to meet him.

"Tom, are you all right? We were . . ."

He nodded. "I'm okay."

"Where were you, boy?" Uncle Carl asked. His voice was quiet and cold in contrast to Aunt Belle's fluttering concern.

Tom looked at his uncle. "Can we talk about it in the car?"

Uncle Carl hesitated, then seemed to sense that Tom was not trying to avoid the consequences of some ordinary mischief, and nodded his agreement.

"I'll have them bring the car around. We've already checked out."

"What's wrong?" Aunt Belle demanded.

Tom avoided her eyes. "We'll talk in the car."

"Tom, you know how I hate a mystery. Don't be so peculiar."

A family with two small children passed them on the way out to the street. "I can't talk here," Tom told her, wishing his aunt for once could be calm and sensible.

She took his arm, her sharp nails digging into his skin. "Something's really wrong, isn't it? I'm sure of it. You've never acted so peculiar before."

Her choice of the word peculiar annoyed him. He pulled away from her and began carrying out their suitcases. Behind him he could hear her taking in deep breaths. He whirled around to glare at her, warning her with his eyes that she must not faint. He was surprised at the anger he felt welling up from deep inside him, more than he would have believed possible.

"Tom," she called.

He hurried outside with the suitcases. The car had just been parked in front of the hotel. Silently, he helped his uncle load their luggage into the trunk, then went back into the lobby after the other bags. Aunt Belle gave him a wounded look as she climbed into the back seat. He felt guilty. As quickly as it had come, his anger had gone, and he had no idea where it had come from.

His uncle drove toward the river. "Where were you off to this morning?" he asked.

"Just exploring." Tom watched the streets flash by. "I meant to be back in plenty of time."

His uncle grunted. He settled his large bulk more comfortably behind the wheel. "I believe you did. Suppose you tell us what you couldn't tell us back there at the hotel."

Tom took a deep breath. "I found some paintings," he began. He was at a loss on how to continue. "I . . ."

Uncle Carl looked at him. "Whatever it is, Tom, remember we're on your side," he said gently. "Now you've never been afraid to talk to us before."

"I know that."

"Then just tell it straight."

"Well, all my life I've had these . . . these visions."

"Visions?" Aunt Belle said from the back, a note of hysteria in her voice. "What do you mean, visions?"

"I don't know what else to call them. Pictures maybe, fantasies, only . . ."

29

"Only what?"

"Belle," Uncle Carl said. "Suppose we let the boy tell it his way." He drove the car onto the highway beside the river. "Go on, Tom."

"They're like . . . memories," he said. "Like somebody else's memories. I never realized this before." A cold sweat had broken out all over his body.

"How can . . ."

"Belle!"

"Well, he's not making any sense, Carl." She leaned forward and squeezed Tom's shoulder. "How can you have someone else's memories?"

Tom turned to look at her. There was something too insistent in her voice, too anxious in her expression.

"Tell us about the paintings," Uncle Carl said. "You mentioned paintings."

Tom faced forward again. "Over on the Common, at the art show, there are three paintings that are exactly like the pictures in my head, the pictures I've told no one about." He nodded, trying hard to find a way to explain it to them. "It's like the artist looked inside my head and painted my private thoughts."

"What sort of thoughts?" Uncle Carl asked.

"A field by the sea, a girl with long, gold colored hair. In the paintings she's playing a guitar. In my mind she's singing, sometimes, only I never hear the words."

Aunt Belle snorted. "Nonsense, Tom. People paint sea-scapes all the time. And lots of girls play guitars. You're seventeen, your imagination . . ."

Tom shook his head. "I'm trying to tell you that what this artist painted is exactly what I've been seeing all my life. Visions, memories, fantasies, whatever the hell you want to call them, her paintings are exact copies!"

30

"Tom, don't swear at me!"

"I'm sorry."

"What's the artist's name?" Uncle Carl asked.

"Sylvia Macy."

During the long silence that followed his telling them about the paintings, Tom sensed much that remained unspoken. "Does that name mean anything to you?" he asked at last.

"No," Aunt Belle said quickly. "Nothing at all."

His uncle glanced at him but remained silent.

"Maybe these pictures, these memories are not someone else's," Tom said. "Maybe they're mine. You took me in when I was little. I had a life before Delmory."

"Tom, you were only a baby when we took custody of you," Aunt Belle said. It sounded to Tom as if she were pleading with him. "We've told you all about it."

"Tell me again."

She was breathing deeply. This time Tom felt no anger. He turned and looked at her. "Tell me again," he repeated gently.

"Well, Carl, this boy . . ." She shook her head when she saw that no help was coming from her husband. "Very well. It's just like we've told you, Tom. Your father and mother were killed in a car accident when you were only a few months old. You were hardly scratched. Your Uncle Carl was your father's only family and since we were your godparents, we naturally . . ." She paused to look angrily at Uncle Carl. "If we'd done what I wanted to do, we would have adopted you outright and never let on to you that you were anything else except our natural offspring."

Uncle Carl said nothing. If he realized she was glaring at him, he pretended not to notice.

31

"How old was I?"

"Oh, let's see. It was a long time ago, you know." She looked out the window beside her, as if to find the answer written on the roadway. "Five, no six months old."

Tom wanted to say you're lying; I know you're lying. But there was no reason to think this, none he could firmly put his finger on.

"So you can see that you couldn't possibly remember anything from back then. All your memories are here with us, in Delmory, not by the sea."

"Then how can Sylvia Macy paint pictures just like the pictures in my head?"

"Tom, I think you're exaggerating," Aunt Belle told him. "They're not that similar, or you both saw the same picture book when you were little or . . . or it's just some damned evil coincidence."

They stopped talking about it then, and the rest of the ride home was in silence. Tom switched places with Uncle Carl and drove part of the way. Several times he noticed his uncle looking at him, and he wanted to say to him, you know more than Aunt Belle is saying, don't you? Tell me what you know. . . .

And when they drove into the familiar driveway beside the familiar house in Delmory, their driveway, their house, it wasn't all that familiar anymore. There was a change. Certainly Tom sensed it, if they didn't.

Crazy as it was to feel this way, he no longer felt at home here. He looked at the house as he and his uncle unloaded the car, and he felt a pang of loneliness.

"Here, Tom," his uncle said. "I'll carry the others."

They walked up the path together, but Tom knew it was not the same. It wasn't home.

Chapter Four

SUNDAY NIGHT Tom slept fitfully, drifting in and out of
dreams of endless tunnels, dreams of long, sliding descents
down colorless hills. At four he sat up and read for a while;
before breakfast he quietly went downstairs and let himself
out onto the front porch. Monday morning greeted him
fresh and wet under a heavy dew. His feet made perfect
footprints on the lawn.

At Wayne's house he hesitated. No one was up yet. He
circled behind the house and called under Wayne's window. When that didn't work, he threw pebbles at the
screen.

But it was another upstairs window that opened. Wayne's
mother looked down at him.

"Good morning, Tom. Do you want Wayne?"

Tom winced. "Sorry, Mrs. Bessier. Yeah, if you don't mind waking him."

"No trouble, Tom. Is something wrong?"

Tom shook his head.

"Are you sure? You look quite pale. Or is it the morning light?"

"Must be the light."

"I'll get Wayne."

Tom walked around to the driveway and sat on a wagon belonging to Wayne's kid brother. A car backed out of the driveway across the street and drove off, trailing a cloud of exhaust fumes.

Wayne came out tucking his shirt into his jeans. He hadn't combed his hair. "What's happening?"

Tom stood up, catching the wagon before it fell over.

"Walk me to the corner."

"What's the matter, Tom?" Wayne's face showed concern. "Why don't you come in and have some breakfast and we'll . . ."

"Don't have time." Tom started walking down the driveway. "Coming?"

Wayne fell in beside him and they walked together out to the street and turned right.

"I need you to cover for me again at the drugstore."

Wayne stared at him. "You didn't get me out of bed to ask me that, did you? For Christ's sake, Tom. I was dreaming about Cheryl Babcock."

"Sorry." Tom slowed down as they neared the corner. "I couldn't wait around to ask you later. I have to leave early today."

"Where to?"

"I'm hitching to Boston."

"Boston. You just came back, didn't you?"

"Yeah."

"I can't figure you out, Tom." They stopped at the corner and faced each other. A bus backfired at it passed them. "Why don't you tell me what the hell . . ."

"Look Wayne, I can't explain now. I can't work tonight. I don't know when I'll get back from Boston. Will you cover for me or won't you?"

"Olson is a pain in the ass."

"So forget it. To hell with the job." Tom started walking away.

"Wait up, will you?" Wayne ran after him. "Of course I'll work. What are friends for, for Christ's sake? But you'll owe me."

Tom grinned at him. "I'll owe you."

Wayne studied him. "And you're not going to tell me what this is all about?"

Tom shrugged. "Not now."

"Okay, but you got me worried, buddy."

"Don't worry. Just lend me ten dollars."

"Ten?"

"Yeah, I'll pay you back tomorrow, if I'm home."

"I'll have to get my wallet. It's at the house."

They walked together back to Wayne's house and Tom again waited in the driveway. Mrs. Bessier came out on the porch and looked at him.

"I've got sausage frying," she called. "And fresh rolls."

"Sounds great, but I ate already," Tom told her.

"Well, you're not much of a liar, Tom Stevens," she said as she disappeared back into the house.

When Wayne came out with the money, Tom apologized. "Tell your mother I'll be sure to stop and eat next time I come by, okay?"

Wayne nodded. "Want some company?"

Tom shook his head.

"Well, see you."

Tom waved to him from the street, then hurried to the corner. He wanted to get onto the highway before all the Boston-bound commuters were gone.

Delmory was waking up. Tom could smell bacon and coffee as he walked by the houses. Without thinking anything of it, he started singing under his breath:

> I'll dry your tears, baby,
> I'll chase 'way that frown,
> in the morning I'll feed you,
> in the evening go to town . . .
> and buy you a ribbon
> and buy you a toy,
> anything to make you
> my good little boy. . . .

The morning darkened. He stopped short as if the street had dropped into a pit, leaving him teetering at its edge.

The melody of the song belonged to the girl with long, golden hair, but this time the words, her words, had come to him from somewhere so far away that even as he tried to repeat them now, they slipped away in tatters.

He leaned against a section of chain link fence. A dog inside the yard lunged at him but he hardly noticed.

. . .*in the morning I'll feed you, in the evening* . . . Like birds in a storm wind, the words fluttered by him, just out of reach. He closed his eyes tightly and summoned up the picture of the girl, singing, singing, singing in the tall, brown grass, the wind blowing her hair across her face, blowing her hair to one side so that he could see . . .

"Are you all right?"

Startled, Tom opened his eyes. A man carrying a briefcase stood a few feet away, staring at him.

"Are you sick?"

Tom shook his head. "No, I'm . . ."

"Are you stoned?" The man was smiling at him. "Kind of early, isn't it?"

Tom didn't try to explain, but walked away instead. Let the man think whatever he wanted to think. He had to get to Boston; he had to find Sylvia Macy.

He caught a ride with a construction worker already late for a job in Cambridge. They raced through the traffic, breaking every speed limit on the way. In Cambridge beside the subway entrance Tom barely had a chance to get out of the car and call his thanks before the car spun off into traffic again, its rear tires squealing.

Asking questions, Tom found the correct side of the underground station and rode the subway into Park Street. Up above, the Common was crowded with people on their way to work. He crossed the Common, only to find most of the exhibits already torn down, the art show apparently over. Sylvia Macy's paintings were gone.

"I'm looking for some paintings by Sylvia Macy," he asked one of the men tearing down a backdrop. The worker had intense dark eyes. He looked at Tom as if he had intruded on some private meditation.

"Hey man, I just tear things down. I don't dig the art."

Tom looked around at the other workers. "Is there someone in charge?"

The man shrugged toward a van parked nearby. "Try over there."

Tom found a fat man drinking a cup of coffee beside the van, his large buttocks perched on the bumper. "Are you in charge of the crew here?"

The fat man smiled at him, revealing broken teeth. "Depends who sent you."

"No one sent me. I'm trying to locate some paintings that were here yesterday."

"All the paintings are gone. We're just cleaning up."

"I'm trying to get some information on one of the artists."

"Adding to your collection?" The fat man laughed, spraying coffee on Tom's shirt. "Funny, you don't look like no connoisseur."

Tom turned away as the fat man continued to laugh. His arm was nearly jerked off his shoulder.

"Don't be so touchy. I was just teasing you." The fat man pushed himself off the van and waddled to a large trash barrel. He fished around in it for a moment, then brought out a pamphlet and handed it to Tom. "Here. This should give you what you're looking for."

"Thanks." Tom took the pamphlet and glanced at its cover:

Boston Festival of Art

Under this large blue lettering, there was a reproduction of an abstract painting. Leafing through the pages he found no mention of Sylvia Macy or her work. But there were lists of participating donors and galleries in the back, and on the last page he read:

STEERING COMMITTEE
Tanya Walker, Chairperson
The Walker Gallery
Benjamin Tate
Bell Gallery of Fine Art
Jon Whitt Gilly
Gallery Avenue North
Carlylle Childers
The Bradbury Museum

There were longer lists of names under specific commit-tees, but he thought he would do best to start at the top.

"Thanks," he said again to the fat man.

"Don't mention it. Glad I could make your day."

Tanya Walker didn't take calls, at least not calls from strang-ers named Tom Stevens. Benjamin Tate was out of town. The telephone booth was hot, suffocating. Tom could feel his face getting red when Jon Whitt Gilly himself answered on the fifth ring.

"Gallery Avenue North, Jon Gilly."

Tom took a deep breath. He hoped this time he wouldn't sound so nervous.

"I'm trying to locate an artist who had three paintings at the art show on Boston Common."

"To buy, I hope." Jon Whitt Gilly sounded surprisingly young.

"No, these paintings weren't for sale. I just need to . . . find the person who painted them."

"What was the artist's name?"

"Sylvia Macy."

"What made you call me?"

"I found your name in the back of the Festival of Art pamphlet."

"Oh, the brochure."

"Yeah."

"Have you tried to narow it down to one of the individual committees?"

"I don't know which one." Tom wiped sweat out of his eyes and opened the door a crack. "There are a lot of names."

"Yes, there are."

"Does her name mean anything to you at all?"

"Sylvia Macy?"

"Yeah."

"Rings a faint bell. What school?"

"I . . ."

"What kind of paintings were they? Abstract, Impressionist, Pop, Op, watercolor, oil?"

"They looked like things really look."

Jon Whitt Gilly laughed. "Wait a minute."

The phone line hummed faintly in Tom's ear while he waited. Outside the booth, a jackhammer started pounding. Tom closed the door again.

"Hello?"

"I'm here."

"Try Alice Blake. She headed up the committee selecting work from the more traditional artists. She runs the Blake Gallery on Newbury Street. Where are you calling from?"

"Across from the Common."

"You're practically there. Newbury runs parallel to Commonwealth, above the Public Gardens. Do you want the telephone number?"

Tom was wilting in the heat inside the booth. "No thanks. I'll walk."

"Your best bet is to see if she can give you more information. All right?"

"Yes. Thanks a lot, Mr. Gilly."

"No trouble." The line clicked as he hung up.

Tom pushed his way out of the phone booth and headed toward the Public Gardens. He was nearly to the swan boats when he remembered the pile of change he had left on the shelf under the phone.

He ran back, but it was already gone.

Chapter Five

THE BLAKE GALLERY was squeezed between a bookstore and a small pub. The hardwood floor reflected the many colors of the paintings hanging on the gallery's walls, the green of the plants in its front windows. Tom asked for Alice Blake, expecting a refusal, an excuse, wondering how insistent he could be. Instead, the girl he spoke to smiled at him and told him to wait.

"Ms. Blake is on the phone. I'll tell her you're here. Your name?"

"Tom Stevens."

"There's coffee on the desk, if you'd like some."

While he waited, Tom fixed himself a cup of coffee in a throwaway cup. His hands trembled slightly as he added sugar. He was hungry and regretted skipping breakfast. It was nearly noon and his head was as light as a balloon. . . .

"Yes, Mr. Stevens?"

He turned and saw a very attractive woman in a light summer suit walking toward him from a doorway in the back of the gallery. Tall, elegant, cool-looking despite the heat of the day, she was older than any woman he had ever thought pretty before. Her blond hair was piled up above her neck and pinned there with two silver combs, a style he didn't particularly like.

"You wanted to see me?"

He had lost his place among his thoughts. His head felt large, off balance.

"I'm . . ." He put down his empty coffee cup and watched her face begin to spin. Then it was he who was spinning as the bright hardwood floor came up and hit him in the chin. He felt someone touching him, felt suddenly cool, deliciously cool. . . .

"Mr. Stevens, are you all right?"

Somehow she had placed a cushion under his head without his knowing it. He realized he had fainted. "I'm sorry," he mumbled.

"Oh, don't be. I don't usually have such a devastating effect on people when I first meet them, but it's really quite flattering."

Her voice was soft, sort of gently teasing. She helped him get to his feet.

"You're not diabetic, are you?"

He started to shake his head, then winced and told her no.

"When was the last time you ate?"

He had to think about it. "Last night."

"Well, no wonder. I thought boys your age ate all the time." She reached for her purse. "Come on, I was just thinking about lunch myself."

42

Outside, the air was a little fresher. He took several deep breaths. He realized she was still looking at him with concern.

"I'll be all right. I just wanted to ask you about . . ."

"We'll discuss it over lunch," she interrupted and led the way into the pub next door.

Their table was in a corner by a brick wall. The pub was dimly illuminated by several brass ship's lights and by reflections from the mirror behind the bar. Everyone there seemed to know Alice Blake; their lunch order was taken immediately.

As he sipped a Coke, Tom looked around at the other tables. "It's nice in here," he said.

"Feeling better?"

"Yeah, I'm okay. Sorry about being such a . . ."

She reached over and covered his mouth with her fingers. "Forget it. I once fainted during the middle of a violin recital, on a stage in front of a couple hundred people." She laughed. "Almost impaled myself on my bow."

When his roast beef sandwich came, she looked up from her salad several times to watch his progress. He tried to eat slowly, but he was too hungry. She signaled the waiter.

"The young man would like another of the same."

"No, I don't have enough money for two."

"He'll have it anyway," she told the waiter, who nodded with a small dip of his head and departed toward the kitchen. "This is my treat, Tom."

"No, I can . . ."

"I insist. I'll deduct it as a business expense. Afterall, you are a customer."

"But I'm not."

She winked at him. "Well, we'll call you one anyway."

"I'm trying to locate an artist who had three paintings at

43

the art show on the Common. Jon Whitt... Mr. Gilly suggested I ask you about her."

Alice Blake sipped from her wine glass. "What's her name?"

"Sylvia Macy."

"Why are you looking for her?"

Tom quickly explained his link to the paintings he had seen yesterday in the exhibit on the Common. He tried to make it clear to her that the similarity between his images and these paintings was too close to be coincidental.

"How fascinating!" she exclaimed. "So these three paintings could have come right out of your own head?"

He nodded. "Particularly two of them, the two of the field by the sea."

"ESP? Possession? Some dark, supernatural, scary thing like that?"

He shrugged. "More like memories."

"How do you mean? Do you remember that field by the sea?"

His second sandwich came. He took a large bite and chewed slowly while he thought. Finally he shook his head. "I don't remember the field by the sea. The pictures in my head are like memories, but they don't connect to any other part of my life. It's like they're someone else's memories."

"I love it," Alice Blake said. She ordered another glass of wine. "So we're back to possession, to something supernatural."

"I just don't know." Tom put up his hands. "I was orphaned when I was a baby. My aunt and uncle raised me. But it happened when I was so young that for me to remember anything from back then would be impossible, unless..."

"Unless what?"

44

"Unless they're lying to me."

"Do you think they are?"

"I can't believe they would, and yet . . ."

"And yet you wonder."

The gentle sympathy in her voice made him look at her. "Yeah, I wonder."

She reached across the table and squeezed his hand. "And Sylvia Macy is the key."

"She has to be. She shares these thoughts, these images. She's got to be the one to tell me what they mean."

Alice Blake nodded. "Well, I'm the one who arranged to have her paintings in the show."

Tom stared at her. Around them the pub was filling up for lunch, the buzz of conversation growing louder. "You know her?"

"I did. We handled some of her work several years ago. That's how I knew where to locate the three paintings you saw. I sold them originally."

"Then . . ."

"Let me finish." She pushed away her salad bowl, brought her wine glass exactly in front of her on the table. "When we were planning the art show and what would be included, I badly wanted Sylvia Macy represented, so I tried to track her down. My last contact with her would have been, let's see, over two years ago. But as far as I knew she was still in town and I put out all my feelers."

The waiter brought the check. Alice Blake opened her purse and put down a twenty dollar bill. When Tom reached for his wallet, she shook her head.

"I couldn't find her, Tom. It was as if the earth swallowed her up. So I talked to the people who had purchased those three paintings and convinced them to let me show them.

Sylvia Macy is a major local artist and, even if I couldn't ask her for something directly, I was determined that she be part of the show."

"Maybe she's moved somewhere else, to another city."

Alice Blake shrugged. "I'd know where she is, if she's still painting. She's too good to remain out of sight for long."

"Then you think she's still here in Boston?"

"That would be my hunch. Not painting, for some reason, but here somewhere." The waiter returned with her change. She left a three dollar tip, and they walked out onto the street.

"Where do I start looking?" Tom said, feeling suddenly overwhelmed.

They stopped and faced each other on the pavement in front of her gallery. Alice Blake touched his arm. "I wish I could be more help."

"You've been great. And thanks for lunch."

She smiled. "My pleasure. Promise me you won't skip any more meals."

"I promise."

"Keep in touch? Let me know any progress you make. I might think of something in the next few days."

Tom nodded.

"There is one thing you should know about Sylvia Macy."

"What's that?"

"She had a history of emotional illness. Bouts of depression. She was hospitalized at least once while we were showing her work."

"Do you think that's why she's disappeared?"

"Maybe." Alice Blake smiled and put out her hand. "I've got to get back to the gallery."

He shook her hand and thanked her again. At the gallery door she turned and waved to him.

He walked back to the Public Gardens and sat on a bench. The swan boats were tied up for some reason, although hundreds of people were wandering by. He tried to put everything he had learned from Alice Blake into perspective. In one way, it seemed like a dead end, but on the other hand, he knew much more than he had this morning when he started out. And he had actually tracked down someone who once knew Sylvia Macy.

He had to be encouraged, not discouraged. Finding Sylvia Macy wasn't going to be as easy as he'd first thought. But that was no reason for quitting. He had to keep looking for her. She was still his one link to the answer he longed for: the truth about the field by the sea and the girl with long, golden hair.

He stood up and began to walk toward the river and the long hitch back to Delmory. Around him the city sweltered under the hot afternoon sun. Buildings blocked the sky and flags on high flag poles beat in breezes that did not reach the streets. Car tires squealed, people jostled him, red balloons floated above a souvenir stand.

This was a city he hardly knew, but he would be back, to find its secrets and its answers. He reached the highway by the river, crossed it and stuck out his thumb. I'll be back, he thought. I'll be back, and I'll find you, Sylvia Macy.

Chapter Six

ON THE WAY back to Delmory, Tom lost his ride switching from one highway to another and didn't catch another ride until evening. It was after dark before he walked onto his street in Willow Hill. His feet hurt, his throat was dry, his courage was at a low ebb. It was difficult to recapture the determination he had felt sitting on that bench in the Public Gardens.

He climbed the front steps and slumped into one of the rockers on the front porch. He forced off his sneakers.

"Is that you, Tom?" Aunt Belle called from inside.

"Yeah."

He knew he should have called them when supper time came and he was still on the road. He braced himself for a hassle.

But it didn't come. When he went inside, Aunt Belle was dishing out his supper and Uncle Carl was sitting quietly at the table, sipping a beer.

"I kept it warm," Aunt Belle said as she put down one pot and reached for another. "Your favorite, pot roast with tons of onions."

She looked at him for a second, then looked away, but not before he saw how red her eyes were. "Go wash up," she told him.

They didn't talk about where he'd been until he was finishing his first serving.

"More?" Aunt Belle asked, jumping up from her chair.

He nodded. "I went to Boston."

"We thought you did," Uncle Carl said. "To see if you could find out more about those paintings?"

"Yeah." Tom went to the refrigerator for more Coke and got his uncle another beer while he was there.

"Thanks, Tom." His uncle opened the can and poured the beer into his glass. It formed a large head and he waited for it to subside. "Did you learn anything?"

Tom put his arm around Aunt Belle and made her sit down. "You don't have to wait on me."

She looked flustered. "Well, you're probably hungry and . . ."

"Sit," he said gently.

"Tell us what you found out," she asked.

"I found out that it's going to be a lot harder to find Sylvia Macy than I thought. But I did track down someone who knows her, or knew her up until two years ago. She's dropped from sight." Was it his imagination or did his aunt seem to relax, as if his news of failure had relieved her anxiety?

"So that's that, I guess," Uncle Carl said.

Tom shook his head. "No. I'm going to Boston to stay, for as long as I have to, for as long as it takes me to find her."

"Tom, that's crazy."

"I have to, Aunt Belle. I remembered the words to the song this morning."

Aunt Belle looked at him, then looked down. "What song?"

"The song the girl sings when I think of her. The words came to me this morning. It's a kind of lullaby."

"You remembered?" Uncle Carl said.

Tom nodded. "Yes, I remembered." He looked at them both, fighting back the emotions that welled up inside him. They looked older than they had ever looked before. He loved them so much.

"That's what these things are," he whispered. "Memories. Memories I'm not supposed to have, but I do just the same. And they're getting stronger and clearer all the time." He closed his eyes, dreading what he had to say to them. He plunged ahead. "So I figure you've been lying to me and I'd like you . . ." He cleared his throat. "I'd like you to stop lying and tell me the truth."

In the silent kitchen Tom could hear the ticking of the big grandfather clock in the front hall. He waited, forcing himself to look at Aunt Belle, then at Uncle Carl.

"Please," he said at last.

It was Uncle Carl who relented first. He drained his glass of beer, poured the last drops from the can. "We've got to tell him, Belle. He has a right to know."

"No!"

Uncle Carl shook his head slowly. "It's gone too far now to stop. It's unraveling, Belle, like all falsehoods unravel, sooner or later." He looked at Tom. "It's not so terrible, really. Maybe we should have been honest with you about it from the first. But your aunt felt . . ."

"Sure, blame it all on me." Aunt Belle stared at them, tears streaming down her cheeks. "Blame me."

"I'm not blaming you, Belle," Uncle Carl said gently. "There isn't any issue of blame here. We agreed that lying might be for the best, but we were wrong."

"Tell me," Tom pleaded.

"You have a sister named Sylvia," Uncle Carl told him. "She brought you here when you were five years old. She was fifteen or sixteen then. She left you here one morning early and disappeared. We couldn't find her afterwards. After a while, we stopped looking."

"Why did she bring me here?" Tom had difficulty making his voice loud enough to be heard.

"Because of the fire." Uncle Carl shook his head. "I'll start at the beginning. Your father had problems with the bottle. Your mother did die in that car accident when you were a few months old. But your father lived. And since he was the one driving, we figure he blamed himself for her death. Maybe that was the reason for his drinking, maybe not. We had no idea till afterward just how much he was drinking."

Tom couldn't breathe. "What happened?"

"Your house caught fire and your father burned to death inside it. You and your sister Sylvia got out alive. She must have been in shock. She brought you here all the way from the Cape and . . ."

"Which Cape?"

"Cape Ann. I don't know how she . . ."

"Was our house near Shepherd Island?" Tom demanded.

Uncle Carl looked at Aunt Belle. "I don't know."

"Your house was back from the coast," Aunt Belle said. Tears were still running from her eyes. "In the scrub woods. I don't remember anything about Shepherd Island."

She pulled out her handkerchief and blew her nose. "You see, you wanted to forget. You... you were very upset for days after Sylvia left you here. We had to get Doctor Cote to give you something to calm you down. Oh, you about broke my heart the way you carried on and then..."

"Take it easy, Belle," Uncle Carl said. He got up and fetched her a glass of water, but she stared at it as if it were poisoned.

"Then, Tom," she continued, "you just woke up one morning and... and you were all better. It was awhile before we realized that somehow you had forgotten everything about your father and your sister Sylvia."

"That's when we stopped looking for her," Uncle Carl told him.

"She was gone and you were here with us and we loved you so and the last thing we wanted was to have all that ugly horror come up again. You wanted to forget, Tom. And so we helped you."

Uncle Carl patted her shoulder. "Not such a terrible thing we did, Belle. He'll understand, in time."

Tom stood up. "I want to understand."

"We love you," Aunt Belle said.

"I know. I love you too. This doesn't change that." The kitchen seemed alive with light. It burned his eyes. "Then all these pictures in my head are true ones. They're memories, and Sylvia Macy is really my sister."

Uncle Carl nodded. "If she did those paintings you saw, she must be. Do you still have to find her?"

52

"More than ever. Don't you see?"

Aunt Belle came over and hugged him. "This is your home, Tom, don't forget that."

"I won't."

"Even if you find Sylvia. You belong here with us."

"Don't, Belle," Uncle Carl told her. "Don't tie the boy up in knots."

"Well, are you just going to let him run off to Boston like this? He's only seventeen and . . ."

"Belle, do you really think we can stop him if he wants to go?"

She hugged Tom again, then released him. "No, it's too late to stop anything now." She was crying again.

"I'll always love you," he told them, his voice failing. He ran outside onto the porch to be alone.

During the long night Tom did not think of sleep. He stayed on the porch until his aunt and uncle went to bed, both of them saying good night from the doorway. Every one of his senses was on edge, alert, watchful: he imagined he could feel the earth revolving slowly under him.

He walked the neighborhood, the old neighborhood, his neighborhood, seeing it new in the darkness and shadows. He had come here when he was five years old, with a whole childhood somewhere else, on Cape Ann. His sister had brought him here and left him. . . .

He whirled around, thinking someone had called his name, but the night was empty, the houses on all sides silent and asleep.

Sylvia, fifteen, in shock, bringing him here to leave him with Uncle Carl and Aunt Belle, saying good-by. . . .

He walked around the block again, cut through a vacant lot, came at the house from another angle. Sylvia was the girl with long, golden hair, singing her song through all the times he had remembered her and not even known he was remembering. *I'll dry your tears, baby, I'll chase 'way that frown . . .* Sylvia in the field by the sea, singing her lullaby. He stopped in the middle of the street in front of the house. Singing her lullaby to him! He was a child then, when she was fifteen.

He walked on, out to the corner, down to Kip's Market, remembering how often he had come here for ice cream in past summers but trying now to readjust his memory, trying to realize that all these Willow Hill memories were recent ones, trying to realize that five years of his life had been lived somewhere else with a sister he could only remember faintly and a father who was a total blank.

He wondered if it would all come back to him in time, wondered if he would remember it all, the five lost years he'd spent as someone else's child.

The clock tower in the distant center of town struck the early morning hour. Still he did not go in to sleep but walked instead again and again over the trails and streets he had walked all his years in Willow Hill. He realized he was saying good-by, for he felt himself being swept away by this new truth about himself and he thought he might never find his way back to here, to this safe and happy home.

His aunt and uncle had tried to protect him from a past too painful for him to go on remembering. At five he had found a way to forget. Now, like an old tape recording, rediscovered and about to be replayed, his true past would be revealed.

I'm afraid, he thought. He tried to put the fear away, but it was out in the street with him. Again he thought he heard someone call his name and turning onto the block in front of the house, he remembered.

Sylvia holding his hand until they reached the house and then she let it go and pushed him away saying, *go in, go inside, you have to stay here,* her voice an urgent whisper and he tried to follow her as she left him there and she said *no, you can't go with me, you stay here,* and pushed him again up onto the porch and rang the bell and when there were steps inside, she ran away, her green skirt lashing around her legs and he cried to her, *no, you take me* but she was gone and the door opened. . . .

Tom stood there now in front of that same porch as the memory claimed him like a bird of prey, taking hold of him with a shock, a jolt.

Birds sang in the trees above him; he sought the porch and the rocker like an island at sea and sat there while dawn slowly lightened the eastern sky. Clouds became pink and the birds sang louder, setting up an awful din throughout the neighborhood, as he sat there and wondered if he ever would, ever could, come back to Willow Hill.

Uncle Carl came out onto the porch around five, rubbing his whiskery face, regarding the sky.

"Been up all night?"

Tom nodded.

"Going to Boston today?"

"Yes. I have to take some money out of the bank and tell Mr. Olson I'm quitting my job. Then I'll be going."

"Need anything?" His uncle sat down in the rocker next to his.

"I don't think so."

"You'll call us if you do?"

"Yes."

"Call anyway. Your aunt will be worried."

"Okay." Tom looked at his uncle. "I will."

"Yeah, call often, collect. Let us know when you find Sylvia."

"Can you tell me more about her, and about my father?"

Uncle Carl stood up heavily. "Your aunt stayed up half the night writing you a letter, things she thought you should know about them . . . about your family."

"She did?"

"Yes. She's worried sick about your happiness right now, but she won't try to stop you from going to Boston. So she wrote down things we remembered, things that you have a right now to know. She'll give it to you before you leave."

He walked to the door. "How are you going?"

"Bus, I guess."

"Want us to come see you off?"

Tom thought about it.

"Guess you'd rather not," his uncle said.

"Uncle Carl?"

"What?"

Tom stood up and put out his hand, and his uncle took it and they shook hands slowly.

"You be careful," Uncle Carl said.

"I will."

"Remember, we're only a phone call away."

"I'll remember."

His uncle went back inside. The sun was up. A new day was starting.

Part 2

NIGHTSHOW

Chapter Seven

THE BUS was nearly empty on the ride into Boston. Tom sat by himself near the back, in the privacy of his own thoughts.

"I was going to have to let you go anyway," Mr. Olson had told him at the drugstore. "Because of all the time you've been missing."

Tom looked out the window at the suburban hillsides sweeping by.

"Wayne's a better worker than you," the druggist had added. "Guess I'll offer the job to him."

Tom shook his head. The words still stung him, adding to the guilt he felt over quitting. He hadn't tried to explain why he was leaving Delmory. The look in the druggist's eyes told him the man would not listen to anything he said.

It was done. He would look ahead, to Boston, to finding Sylvia. As the bus plunged on toward the city, Tom read his aunt's letter for the second time:

Dearest Tom,

There's nothing to do now but level with you as best we can and hope you can understand why we kept all this from you. As God is my witness, we weren't trying to win your love by keeping you from remembering your original family. If there had been anything there to be proud of, your Uncle Carl and me would have been the first to remind you of it.

His aunt's handwriting started off neat and precise; as the letter continued, the words became unevenly spaced, the lines themselves began to slant down the page:

Your father's name was Keith Stevens. Never had a nickname, he wasn't the type, somehow, to ever have a nickname hung on him. Truth to tell, and I don't want to hurt your Uncle Carl, who's reading this as I write it, but if we're going to be truthful, I never much liked your father. Too stuck on himself, too uppity, for my taste, with his arty ways, especially for a drunk who kept his children in rags in a shack in the scrub woods. I'm sorry, Tom, but it's true.

The following pages of the letter were more difficult to make out as his aunt's handwriting continued to deteriorate. Had she been writing faster and faster, to get this all down, or was each sentence that much harder to write, that much more painful?

Tom, you're not at all like your father. You remind me of your mother. Her name was Denise—Denny, I called her—and I loved her dearly. She was too young to be married to your father, too fragile. He was a bully even then, before her death gave him an excuse to start his heavy drinking. She loved flowers and her pet canary and he just ran roughshod over her, not at all the sensitive painter everyone thought he was.

Your sister Sylvia was ten years older than you, a little mirror image of your mother, but different too, sadder, deeper. Where your mother bubbled like a brook and tried to laugh at life, even when it did poorly by her, your sister watched it out of those sad, big eyes of hers, taking it all in. Of course, she was still real young when the car accident killed your mother. You were too young then to realize what you'd lost, but Sylvia, she knew. From the stories we heard about your father afterwards, she knew far too much about life for someone so young.

The bus made a stop in front of a garage. Through the window beside him Tom could see a small section of the Boston skyline. A lump of excitement was forming in his stomach. As the bus moved on again, he resumed reading:

I'm not going to repeat rumors here, Tom, especially not rumors about the dead. But the fact is, your father abused you, both you and Sylvia. I hope you never remember that part of it, swear to God, I hope you never do. Your father was a drunken beast, even if people who didn't know better admired his paintings and thought so much of him.

61

Tom, if we'd known what was happening early enough, we would have stepped in, I swear it. But the stories about your father, about his rages and the beatings he inflicted on you and Sylvia and God knows how much of the rest was true, we only learned of it after the fire, after he was dead and Sylvia had brought you to us and disappeared herself, may God bless her wherever she is and forgive us for not searching harder for her. . . .

There was more, but Tom couldn't read it, not now. He stared out the window, thinking of his aunt, remembering how she had pressed the letter into his hands and told him to read it later and wished him well, hugging him, swiping at her tears with her damp handkerchief. And then she had let him go, to walk to the bus station alone, something for which he would be forever grateful.

Boston at four in the afternoon was already spilling over into the streets, thousands of people all going home, wherever home was, like a tide flowing against him. He retrieved his one suitcase, felt for the wallet in his jeans where half his savings now more or less safely resided, and looked around in confusion. For a moment he felt nothing but panic, then he took himself sternly in hand and walked out of the crowds. The first thing to do was find a place to stay.

He bought a newspaper and checked the ads. He knew the hotels were far too expensive, especially since he had no idea how long he would be staying. Apartments he didn't even consider. He couldn't commit himself to anything that permanent, and no one would rent one to someone his age. He had to find a room somewhere, a place he could afford to live in all summer if need be.

The first places he called had no vacancies. Apparently they kept their ads routinely running in the classified, to cover themselves against the random comings and goings of their tenants. Two of the men Tom talked to suggested he call tomorrow; something might open up.

He bought a street map and tracked down two buildings advertised without telephone numbers. The first was too close to a burned-out area. The second, on a side street off Commonwealth Avenue, looked more promising. The landlady, a thin, gray-haired woman with knobby arms, retied her dirty apron and showed him her only available room, on the second floor in the back, overlooking a cement courtyard.

"Thirty-five a week, in advance, plus thirty-five more as a deposit, no cooking, no girls, no music after ten o'clock, you get rowdy I throw you out myself."

He nodded, trying to look as if he knew all about renting a room, as if he'd done it a dozen times before.

"You're kinda young, aren't you?"

"Not really."

"Got a job?"

"Yes," Tom lied. "The room is fine. I'll take it."

The woman grunted, reaching into the pocket of her apron for her receipt book. "Bathroom's down the hall. I'll show you in a sec. Fellow in the room next to this one is a retard, one of them screwballs they're letting roam around loose these days. But he has a job," she glanced at Tom suspiciously, "minds his own business, never a peep out of him which is more than I can say for some of the other charmers I got on my hands."

He paid her for the week plus the deposit. She asked him for his name and made out his receipt. As she handed it to him with two keys, one for his room, the other for the street door, she looked down at his suitcase.

"That all you got?"

"For now."

"Traveling light?"

Tom shrugged.

"Well, come on, Mr. Stevens. I'll show you the john."
She led the way down a dark corridor. The bathroom was
little more than a closet: shower stall, toilet and sink. By the
mirror there was a hand printed card taped on the wall:

THIS IS YOUR BATHROOM.
TREAT IT THAT WAY.

On the door there was another sign:

Guests are responsible for
providing their own toilet
paper and soap.

"Any questions, I'm usually downstairs," the woman told
him as they walked back toward his room.

"Okay. Thank you, Mrs. . . ."

"McDougle. Oh, and one more thing, Mr. Stevens."

He looked at her.

"You want to keep the room after the first week, your
rent is due exactly seven days from right now. I hate to
chase after people."

"No problem."

She laughed. "I wish that was true. I really wish that was
true." She continued to laugh as she descended to the
ground floor.

Inside his room, Tom unpacked his few clothes into the
scarred bureau that leaned against one wall. Outside the
window, three boys were playing basketball in the cement
courtyard. Their voices echoed off other buildings.

Tom lay down on the bed and bunched the single pillow

under his head. Above him the ceiling revealed a road map of tiny lines. It would be easy to get depressed, looking at this small, dingy room that seemed more a part of one of the row houses on Poole Street than a room in one of the most famous cities in the world. He wondered if he should have looked further, but he guessed that given what he could afford, he wouldn't have done better anywhere else.

Outside it was already evening. The basketball bounced across the courtyard and then was still. Somewhere in the distance a siren sounded, grew louder, then faded away. Tom switched on the light over the bed, but it did little to drive away the gathering darkness.

He wasn't here on a vacation, he reminded himself. He was here to find his sister. And maybe he'd get lucky and be out of this room in a week.

Chapter Eight

DURING THE NIGHT Tom woke up with every new sound in his building. Doors slammed, televisions blared, arguments broke out on the floor above him. Tom heard the man Mrs. McDougle had described as retarded come home to the room next to his sometime after midnight. He had a shuffling way of walking—back and forth around his room several times, up and down the hallway to the bathroom twice—that kept Tom awake until the man at last settled down for the night. The last thing Tom heard before he fell soundly asleep was the crash of a bottle breaking in the cement courtyard outside his window.

Mrs. McDougle was sweeping the front steps as he went out in the morning.

"Off to work, Mr. Stevens?"

He nodded. "Yes."

"Nice day," she commented. "But hot."

"Yeah." As he hurried along the street, he could feel her eyes on his back.

Breakfast was eggs, coffee and a Danish at a small restaurant near his room. Then he went to a telephone booth and looked up all the Macys in the phone book. There was no Sylvia Macy listed. Using the change he had asked for at the restaurant, he began calling the numbers one by one. There were twenty-six of them.

Whenever he got an answer, he asked for Sylvia. He received fifteen more or less polite suggestions that he had the wrong number. One Sylvia Macy did come to the phone, but she was sixty-eight and hard of hearing. She had three brothers and two sisters, all living except one, had never painted a picture in her life except those fill-in-the-number kits, but she wished him good luck in finding his sister. She kept him talking as long as she could, finally promising to ask among her family, perhaps he was a long lost cousin, and said good-by twice before she hung up.

The other ten numbers, for whatever reason, didn't answer. He wrote these numbers into a small notebook he had brought from home.

He propped the booth door open to get some air and began searching through the yellow pages, jotting down the addresses of every art gallery listed for the city. He realized he was probably going over territory Alice Blake had already covered, one way or another, when she made her own effort to locate Sylvia, but he had to start somewhere. When he had a list of eighteen places to visit, he got out his new street map, unfolded it against the glass wall of the booth and marked down the galleries he thought he could walk to.

67

He spent the morning going from gallery to gallery, walking to the first half dozen, riding the subway to others, getting lost twice, drawing total blanks in all but two. At these two galleries the person he talked to had heard of Sylvia Macy but had no idea where she was or who was showing her work, if anyone.

He stopped for lunch. When he paid the check, he realized he had to stop eating out and start making his own sandwiches; otherwise his money would continue to melt away.

All afternoon he visited the galleries on his list. The last one brought him back near Newbury Street and when he had again turned up nothing, he walked around the corner to the Blake Gallery and asked the girl there if Alice Blake was in. The girl recognized him from his first visit.

"You're the boy who fainted," she said. Her heavy make-up gave her eyes a surprised look.

"Yeah."

"Sorry!" she said archly. "I'll tell Ms. Blake you're here."

While he waited Tom had sudden doubts about coming here again. Alice Blake had been kind to him on Monday, taking him to lunch, sharing all her information about Sylvia, going out of her way to help him, but . . .

"Tom."

He turned and saw Alice Blake in the doorway at the back of the gallery. "I'm sorry to bother you again. I . . ."

"Come into my office."

As he walked in, she made a halfhearted effort to straighten out her desk, then smiled at him and gave it up. "I'm not a neat person. No, sit in the good chair," she added, indicating a stuffed chair against one wall. Sunlight streamed in from a pair of high windows above an antique oak cabinet. An air conditioner in one wall hummed softly. "So, are you still looking for Sylvia Macy?"

He nodded. "I moved into town yesterday."

Her eyebrows lifted slightly. "Did you? Where are you staying?"

"I've got a room on Turnbull Street, near Commonwealth Avenue."

"Yes, I know the area. It's kind of tacky, isn't it?"

He smiled. "Tacky's one word for it."

She laughed. "But you love it, am I right? Your first place of your own, your first place away from home."

He shrugged. He realized she was gazing intently at him and he hid his embarrassment by looking around her office. Several large photographs of city scenes were hung on the white walls, framed in chrome.

"A friend of mine took those. He's quite talented, don't you think?"

"Yes."

"Well, tell me what progress you've made." She leaned back in her chair. A wisp of her blond hair had come loose and lay across her eyes. She blew it away with pursed lips. "Any luck?"

Tom thought back over all that had happened, then realized that she couldn't know what he had learned when he got home Monday night.

"It's something big, isn't it?" Alice Blake asked softly.

He nodded. "My aunt and uncle finally told me the truth. I was orphaned at five, not when I was a baby. My sister Sylvia brought me to Delmory and left me with my aunt and uncle after our father died in a fire. So Sylvia Macy has to be my sister Sylvia. Her paintings prove it."

Alice Blake sat up straight. "I had a hunch she might be your sister, especially when you told me you wondered if your aunt and uncle were lying to you." She shook her head. "God, you must feel . . ."

He looked away. "Yeah, I do."

"Should I have shared my hunch with you?" she asked. "Would it have made it easier when they told you? God, Tom, I'm sorry I didn't . . ."

He read the pain on her face and it surprised him. "Don't be sorry."

She brushed the wisp of hair out of her eyes again. "Well, it was just a hunch, then, and I didn't want to put ideas in your head that might turn out to be false."

"It's okay. They were upset when they told me. I was upset too."

"You have a right to be."

"Not with them." He wanted to make it very clear to her that he didn't blame Aunt Belle or Uncle Carl. "Not with them," he repeated.

"Sure." She fumbled aimlessly with some papers on her desk. "You must have suppressed it all," she said at last.

He looked at her.

"Suppressed your memories. Blanked them out."

He nodded.

"And nothing's come back?"

"A little." He cleared his throat.

"Well," she said. She smiled at him. "What do you do next?"

"I've been visiting all the galleries I can find, hoping to turn up someone who knows where Sylvia is. I know you already . . ."

She shook her head. "You don't have to apologize to me for being thorough. You have a real need to find her and I didn't, at least not such an urgent one. I might have missed something."

"You didn't, I guess. Not in the places I checked today."

"But you're here for the long haul, right?"

He nodded.

"So one day means nothing." She snatched at the loose end of hair and tucked it up where it belonged. "Are you available for socializing? Or do you plan on searching for your sister night and day?"

He shrugged. "I don't . . ."

She smiled. "I'm asking if you want to have dinner with me."

"Tonight?"

She nodded. "Unless you have other plans."

"I don't have any plans." He felt out of his depth, tried to meet her eyes, then realized he was blushing.

She stood up and came around her desk. Her hand was cool and light on his arm. "I'll pick you up at eight o'clock. What number is your building on Turnbull Street?"

"I don't remember."

"Some detective you are." She walked with him out into the gallery. "Be out in front of your building at eight. I'll find you. Now split. I have an appointment with a rich client in ten minutes."

On his way out the door Tom passed Alice Blake's assistant watering geraniums in a basket on the sidewalk. She grinned at him wickedly and winked.

"She drives a red Fiat Spider. You'll love it."

Before going back to his room, Tom bought a card with an envelope and a stamp in a small stationery store and sat on a bench to write Wayne a quick note:

Dear Wayne,

I'm living in Boston. Found out I have a sister I didn't know about and I'm trying to find her. It's a long story. I'll explain when I see you. I dropped by your house Tuesday but you weren't there and I didn't

71

have time to come out to the lake. Sorry I missed you.

Did Mr. Olson give you my job? Don't mention it, you deserve it.

Hang in there,

Tom

He started to seal up the envelope, then stopped and took a ten dollar bill from his wallet and slipped it into the card. He addressed the envelope, stuck on the stamp and crossed the street to a mailbox. He shook away the pang of homesickness that came over him then by running back to his room, in and out of the shadows that cut the streets into slices.

As he was unlocking his door, the door to the room next to his opened and someone stared out at him from the darkness inside.

"Hi," Tom said. "I'm Tom Stevens."

The figure leaned forward slightly. Tom caught a glimpse of a round face, thick lips, puffy cheeks, hair so short he thought at first the man was bald.

"Mr. St. Croix."

Tom turned his key but didn't go in. "You're Mr. St. Croix?"

"Mr. St. Croix."

"I'm Tom Stevens," Tom repeated. "I guess we're neighbors."

"I have a job," the man said. His voice was flat, his words half formed. Tom had to strain to catch them. "I have a job," the man said again.

Tom nodded. For a brief moment he wondered if Mrs. McDougle was hovering somewhere close by, trying to catch him in his lie about having a job of his own. As Tom started into his room, the man coughed.

"Paul St. Croix. Pretty name."

"Yes, it is." In Tom's room a breeze strayed through his open window, billowing the curtains.

"I have a job but today is my day off."

"Where do you work?"

After a long pause, Paul St. Croix answered. "In the kitchen. El Shibar Steak Pit. You eat there?"

"No, I haven't yet."

"Good food, good food. I clean up mostly, wash dishes. Sometimes they tell me do salads."

"Where is it?" Tom waited, then rephrased his question. "Where is the El Shibar Steak Pit?"

"On Boylston."

"I'll have to try it." Tom was eager to be alone, yet felt guilty over his impulse to duck away from Paul St. Croix.

"Cheap. You can af. . .af. . .afford it."

Tom grinned. "Do I look that poor?"

The man stepped back into his shadowy room. "Next time I have my day off, we can talk again. Okay?"

"Sure."

"Okay?"

"Yes, we'll talk again."

"I get every Wednesday off. Every Wednesday."

"Maybe I'll see you during the week."

Paul St. Croix didn't reply to this. He had moved further back into his room, but he still looked out through the open doorway. Tom realized at last that he had been dismissed. He nodded and escaped into his own room.

At a quarter to eight, Tom was out on the front steps waiting for Alice Blake. He had shaved and showered, put on his one pair of cords and his jacket. He felt his heart pulsing in his throat. He wiped his sweaty hands on his trousers.

Evening was falling on the city, on the buildings above

73

him and on Turnbull Street. The neon sign above the bar on the near corner flashed its message: SCHLITZ... SCHLITZ . . . SCHLITZ.

He watched people walk by. Through the open door behind him, he heard Mrs. McDougle come out of her apartment on the ground floor and begin talking to one of the other tenants on the stairs. Secretly, he watched the cars flash by up on Commonwealth Avenue.

He had no watch, only his alarm clock back in his room, but as the minutes slipped by and it became clear that Alice Blake was late, then very late, he decided she had had second thoughts about their dinner date. He tried to hide his disappointment from himself by planning his evening without her: dinner somewhere inexpensive, then maybe a movie.

A car horn blared. He looked up as a red sports car slid to a stop in the street in front of him. Its top was down; Alice Blake was behind the wheel.

"Well, are you going to get in or just sit there admiring my car?"

He stood up and crossed the sidewalk. As she leaned over to unlock his door, her bracelets flashed in the light from the dashboard.

"If you're real good," she said, "maybe I'll let you drive it."

Chapter Nine

THEY WENT to a restaurant called Rainbow's End, in a hotel overlooking the river. Tom felt uneasy in his casual clothes as they followed the maitre d' through the crowded restaurant to their table.

"There's a secret to it, Tom," Alice Blake whispered, guessing his discomfort. "You act as if you dressed correctly for the occasion and everyone else made a perfectly dreadful mistake."

Their table had a view of the buildings downtown, the lights of the airport beyond. Looking out, Tom felt as if he were floating in some nebulous middle ground, not quite part of the sky, not part of any solid building, either.

Alice was smiling. "It's called personal style. If you have a strong enough sense of it, you could walk in here wearing overalls and carry it off."

He looked across the candles at her. She was wearing a blue dress, an opal pendant on a silver chain. "I'm still the worst dressed man in here." He had almost said boy.

She shook her head. "No, Tom, you're the only man who knew it was supposed to be casual." She glanced out the wall of glass. "There's another restaurant at the top of this building. Now *that's* formal. But this is nicer. Less showy, more intimate. Perfect for us tonight."

When their wine came, she proposed a toast to the view. "What do you think of Boston?" she asked.

"Love it."

She smiled. "Me too. That's why I thought the least I could do on one of your first nights here was to take you out and wine you and dine you and show you the sights. Did you think me forward, asking you?"

He shook his head. "No."

"A boy, excuse me, a man like you must get a lot of propositions."

"Not really."

She raised her eyebrows slightly. "Really? I would have thought you had to beat the girls off with a stick."

He grinned, thinking of Wayne calling him socially retarded. "Doesn't seem to work that way."

She brought her wine glass to her lips, sipped slowly, regarded him over the top of the glass. Her eyes made him self-conscious and he looked down at his menu.

"Expensive," he said.

"Order what you like," she told him. "I have an account here." She winked at him. "Too many long, long lunches meant to jolly up fat cat clients with wine and merry repartee."

The waiter came and took their order. Alice Blake refilled their wine glasses. The city flickered beyond the glass wall, its inscrutable patterns of light.

Over dinner he told her the details of what he had learned from Aunt Belle and Uncle Carl Monday night. He recited to her what he could remember now of the words to Sylvia's song and shared with her his guess that it was a lullaby Sylvia had sung to him when he was little.

"You must be angry that they lied to you for so long."

"Well, they lied, Ms. . . . ."

"Alice."

He nodded. "They lied, Alice, but they only did it to protect me, as they saw it."

"Most lies are to protect someone."

"I know." He felt the need to defend his aunt and uncle, make her understand the bond between the three of them. "I don't blame them for it. They thought they were doing the right thing."

"But they kept you from your past, made you think those images you had were something crazy, something that couldn't make sense. If you hadn't seen Sylvia's paintings, you might have gone your entire life hiding those bits and pieces as if they were something to be ashamed of, not even realizing they were memories."

She reached across the table and squeezed his hand. "Memories you have a right to."

It was hard to deny what she was saying. "I think I would have realized the truth about myself sooner or later."

"Do you?" Alice picked up a shrimp tail and pried out the last morsel. "Do you really?"

Tom shrugged. "I guess I don't really know." He cut another slice from his steak. "But I must have wanted to blank it all out myself when I was a kid."

"Sure, when you were five and didn't know any other way to deal with the pain of it. You're not trying to tell me that the decision you made as a lost little five-year old is the same as their decision to deceive you?"

"They didn't deceive me. They protected me. They thought they had to. Besides, they didn't know I was having flashbacks. I hid that from everyone."

She looked at him and smiled. "You're sweet. I like the way you defend them. Loyalty is rare these days."

"Sorry, I didn't mean to sound . . ."

"Don't apologize. It's all right. I was out of bounds anyway." She looked at him more closely. "What's the matter, Tommy?"

"Nothing. I was thinking."

"About?"

He shrugged, decided to tell her. "While I was wandering around Monday night after they went to bed, I remembered Sylvia bringing me there when I was five. She rang the bell and ran off when we heard someone coming. She . . ." Tom took a quick drink of wine, choked, picked up his napkin. "It keeps coming back to me, a dozen times a day, for no reason. It just pops up and there it is, me and Sylvia on that porch twelve years ago. . . ."

He looked at his plate. When he looked up again, he was surprised see tears in her eyes.

"There's so much I don't remember," he told her. "That's what scares me. All the unknown pieces. I don't remember one percent of . . . of what I should remember."

"It's hard for you, Tommy," Alice said. "I can guess how scary it must be, not knowing what else is hidden back there."

"That's it," he said. "Except I know it's got to be bad, or else I wouldn't have forgotten it all."

She shook her head. "Not all bad, Tommy. Some good things must have got buried with the bad."

"You think so?"

"Your love for Sylvia, for one thing. It's plain to me from

what little you've told me that she was a big piece of your world, back then." Alice picked up her wine glass and tapped it against his. "Another toast," she said. "To Tommy finding his Sylvia, and getting right with his past."

They sipped their wine together.

"You knew Sylvia," he said over coffee and dessert. "Tell me about her."

"I didn't know her well, Tommy."

"Well, what you knew of her." He smiled. "It's got to be more than I know."

"She came around one day with some work. I liked it and agreed to show some of her paintings. I sold a few, she came to a couple of parties at the gallery, we talked about the possibility of a one-woman show." Alice shrugged. "I didn't really get to know her well. She was, how shall I put it? She was a very aloof person. Her smiles didn't carry much conviction. She'd look at me when I talked with her, but it was always as if she were seeing something else." Alice laughed. "Typical artist—spacey, self-absorbed, ultimately an enigma."

"What did she look like?"

Alice studied his face. "I can't look at you and recall a family resemblance. But that's not fair—I wasn't looking for one then. Her hair was lighter than yours, more of a brown with gold highlights. She wore it short when I knew her. Very pale complexion, big, expressive eyes, wide mouth, like yours."

Alice stopped. "That's right. You both have the same mouth. She also had . . ." Alice reached across the table and took one of his hands. "Her hands were too large for the rest of her; she really wasn't very tall or big or anything. But her hands were like yours: long fingers, heavy, strong palms." She didn't release his hand. "But they could move so delicately whenever she would make a point in conversation. She talked with her hands."

"It's strange," Tom said. "This is the first real . . ." He paused.

"Evidence that she's really your sister?"

"Yeah. I mean, your description, especially the ways we're the same, it makes her come alive for me. In my flashbacks she's a young girl, but that was twelve years ago."

"And she's how old now?"

Tom thought for a moment. "She's twenty-seven."

"That's another thing about her. When I knew her, she did not come across as a young person. I took her to be in her thirties, even then. She seemed weary somehow, much traveled, if you understand what I mean."

Tom shrugged. "But we have the same hands?"

Alice nodded. "The same hands. Good, kind, gentle hands."

He looked at her.

"Come on," she said. "I'll get the waiter to bring the check. We'll fly from here. The night is just coming alive."

They drove through the streets of Boston in her red Fiat; the lights they passed blurring in Tom's wine-glazed vision. There was another question he wanted to ask Alice, but he couldn't find it in the jumble inside his head. She took him around the Common twice, through Beacon Hill, along the river. The air blew over them through the open top of the car. She drove recklessly but well, taking the corners with a squeal of tires, a snappy downshifting of gears.

"Don't you love it?" she shouted above the noise of the engine. "Don't you just love this town? I like to drive around at night and pretend it's my town, that I own it, that I'm royalty or something." She laughed and looked at him. "Now don't go telling people about my secret fantasies. I have my image of ice bitch to live up to."

She took him to a bar downtown where they had more wine. He was beginning to lose track of the edges of things. It was all a happy blur: the night outside, the dimly-lighted bar, the bright, crystal carafe of wine between them on the table, all a happy blur except for the question nagging him, demanding to be asked if only he could remember it. . . .

Alice tapped his glass with hers. "Sylvia's here, Tommy. You'll find her."

He remembered what he wanted to ask about then: the ugly question that couldn't be ignored.

"Alice, listen to me." He felt the need to alert her to the fact that he was asking something important. His tongue was clumsy and thick.

"What is it, dear Tommy?" She gazed at him with exaggerated attentiveness.

"You told me Monday that Sylvia had some kind of emotional illness. You said she was hospitalized once because of it."

Alice nodded.

"What if she's in a hospital now or a sanatorium or something like that? Wouldn't that account for her disappearance?" He wanted to add the real question: What if Sylvia was truly sick? What if she was out of his reach, even if he found her?

Alice seemed to read his mind and her happy mood evaporated. "They can do wonderful things for depression these days," she told him gently. "And she was perfectly okay most of the time I knew her. She was really out of it just once that I know of, and then only for a little while."

"But she could have got worse. She could be hidden away in some back ward."

Alice shook her head. "No, that's too terrible. Besides, it doesn't happen that way anymore. People are cured these days." She put down some money and took his hand. "Come on. Let's get out of here."

Outside, the street was empty. Tom realized that hours had slipped away. In the car, Alice sat quietly behind the wheel, not starting the engine.

"I have a friend on the police force. He's in administration but he has connections. If you want, I'll have him make some inquiries." She turned in her seat to face him. "Dear Tommy, are you sure you want to know, if she's really ill?"

He nodded.

"Of course you do. I would too, if I were you. No matter what I found." She started the engine, waited for it to smooth out. "I'll talk to my friend then. If Sylvia is in any of the mental institutions around here, he should be able to locate her." Alice shook her head. "What a double bind. You want to find her, but in this case you've got to hope nothing turns up."

She stepped down hard on the gas, spinning the tires as the car fishtailed out into the street.

She drove aimlessly for more than an hour. They didn't talk. It was as if she were trying to make up her mind about something. Finally she pulled the car to a stop and he recognized Turnbull Street, the steps up to his building, to his gray room.

She switched off the engine. "We're here, Tommy," she whispered, as if she believed he had fallen asleep. "Home again, home again . . ."

He fumbled for the door latch, couldn't find it, started climbing out over the side.

"Wait a second, Tommy."

He stopped, balanced on top of the door.

"You know where I am," she said. "Anytime you need me."

He nodded. "Thank you, Alice." He wished his head would clear, wished the wine would go away now and let him find something right to say. "Thank you for dinner," he said finally. "It was a great night."

"Wasn't it," she agreed. Her voice was low.

He started to fall off his perch on the top of the door. He swung his legs the rest of the way over and stood up. When he turned to say good night, she reached up and pulled him down by his jacket lapel. She planted a firm kiss on his mouth.

"I'm in the book, if the gallery's closed," she said. She started the engine and roared off toward Commonwealth Avenue. He watched until the red taillights of her car winked out as she disappeared around the far corner.

Chapter Ten

He met Paul St. Croix in the hallway outside his room the next morning. The man was on his way to the bathroom, a towel around his neck.

"Say, friend," Paul St. Croix said. "Nice day."

Tom nodded. "Looks like." They slipped by each other in the narrow corridor.

"Go there yet?"

Tom stopped. "What?"

Paul St. Croix's features appeared more distorted in the brighter light of morning. Now his mouth began to twitch.

"I didn't understand what you asked," Tom said gently. "Did I go where?"

"El Shibar. Where I work."

"No, not yet. But I will."

"You do. You do, but I'll be in the kitchen."

Tom looked at him. "I'll still know you're there."

Paul St. Croix smiled. He nodded his head vigorously. "I'll be there, you'll be there. I'll be there, you'll be there."

"That's right."

Paul St. Croix raised his hand, pointing a stubby finger at Tom. "Tonight!"

Tom laughed. "Okay, tonight."

"Shake."

Tom put out his hand and Paul St. Croix took it. They shook hands. Tom nodded. "I've got to go."

"Okay. Don't forget."

"I won't."

Outside, the sky was hazy, the morning already warm. Tom bought an orange and two doughnuts and ate his breakfast in the Public Gardens. He had a whole day of gallery hunting ahead of him, but while he ate he allowed himself to replay his evening with Alice Blake. On a fresh page in his notebook he wrote her name in capital letters:

ALICE BLAKE

Under it, he wrote a small list:

> *call her?*
> *flowers?*
> *lunch?*
> *something, but what?*

He laughed at himself and across the bottom of the page he wrote in even bigger letters:

BE COOL

At the nearest telephone booth he made a second list of art galleries, the ones he hadn't visited yesterday, the ones farthest away from the center of the city. Today's list was longer than yesterday's. Using the map, he grouped them as best he could by districts. It would take him two days to reach them all, maybe longer.

Then, on an impulse, he called Aunt Belle collect.

She answered on the third ring. He waited impatiently for the operator to ask her if she would accept the call.

"Yes, of course," she said. "Tom?"

"Go ahead," the operator said, but Tom was already talking.

"I'm not calling too early?"

"No, of course not. But you missed your Uncle Carl. He just left for the store."

"How are you"

"Me? I'm fine. It's you we're worried about."

"Don't be."

"We are."

"I'm doing all right. Got a place to stay."

"What's the address?"

"Turnbull Street, right in town." He looked into his notebook and gave her the street number, which he had jotted down this morning on his way out. "Room 2C."

"Is it a nice place?"

"Great," he lied. "Really nice. Neat, clean, good people."

"Not too expensive?"

"No."

"So, what are you up to?"

"Right now I'm checking all the art galleries, trying to find one where Sylvia might be showing her work."

"Nothing yet?"

"I only started looking yesterday."

"How long . . ." Aunt Belle stopped.

"Until I find her."

"I know." There was a long pause. "We miss you."

86

"Miss you too." It was becoming hard to talk. "Look, I don't want to run up your phone bill. I'll call you again over the weekend."

"Be careful, Tom."

"I will."

"Was the letter any help? Did it answer any of your questions?"

Tom thought about the things she'd written: *Your father was a drunken beast. . . . God knows how much of the rest was true. . . . If there had been anything there to be proud of. . . .*

"Tom?"

"Yeah, it helped."

"It was hard to write."

"I know." He thought she was crying. "I have to get started. I have a long day ahead of me."

"Good-by, Tom."

"Good-by." He hung up, glanced at his notebook and map and headed for the first gallery on his list.

He was slowly learning his way around Greater Boston. The subway lines and the trolleys began to make sense after a while; the buses were another story. He got lost so often that by lunch time he was ready to chuck it in and flag down a cab, hire it for the day. If he could only afford to.

Then in Brookline, at exactly ten minutes after one, he had his first bit of luck.

The Gallery American occupied the second floor of a yellow brick building that had recently been renovated with new steel-framed windows and impressive glass doors. The man he talked to smiled the moment he mentioned Sylvia's name.

"Yes, Sylvia Macy, wonderful artist. So much feeling."

"Then you know her?" Tom couldn't keep the excitement out of his voice.

The man wore a tweed jacket and looked hot. He guided Tom to one side as a door opened and two workmen came through carrying a large crate.

"Take it back into the storeroom," he told them.

"Do you know her?" Tom asked again.

"I do, or I did. We had several of her paintings here a few years ago before she got high priced and moved her work in town. Are you looking for something of hers to buy? I don't mean to be rude, but I don't think you can afford her now. I can't afford her now."

Tom looked around the gallery, trying to hide his disappointment. "How long since you've seen her?"

The man in the tweed jacket considered, running one finger along his lower lip. "Three years, maybe four."

Another cold trail, not even as fresh as the one Alice had provided him with.

"Are you looking for her?"

Tom nodded. "Yes, I am. Not her paintings, her."

"Why ever, if I may be so personal?"

Tom shrugged. "I think she's my sister."

"And you . . ."

"I haven't seen her since I was five." Tom took a deep breath. "And you wouldn't have any idea where she might be?"

The man shook his head. "Not a clue."

Tom thanked him and started out. The man called him back.

"If you haven't seen her since you were . . ."

"Five."

The man nodded. "Then you don't know what she looks like. You could walk right by her and never know it."

"I guess."

"Well, then I *can* help you." He told Tom to wait and disappeared into a back office. When he reappeared ten minutes later, he was carrying a piece of drawing paper.

"Took me awhile to find it. I was going to have this framed, but I never did." He pushed it at Tom. "It's a nice likeness. One of our other artists did it, right here at an opening she came to."

Tom took the sheet of paper. On one side above some scribbles there was a pencil sketch of a woman with short hair, large, wide-open eyes, a full mouth. The drawing was smudged, the face unfamiliar; he had a difficult time matching it to the description Alice had given him last night over dinner.

He reminded himself that the woman Sylvia had become was not the person he knew. He looked for the girl he did remember, the girl with long, golden hair in the field by the sea; and he thought he saw her, fleetingly, there in the drawing, looking back at him for just an instant. . . .

"I don't know why I kept it," the man in the tweed jacket was saying. "Sentimental reasons, I guess."

Tom looked up from the drawing and realized the man was staring at him.

"You see, I had a crush on your sister back then." He laughed uncomfortably, as if the memory were a painful one. "Not that she often noticed me. She was very much, well, into herself. Very wrapped up in her own head. Didn't pay much attention to . . ." He let his sentence drop. "She was center stage in her own drama, though, whatever that was."

"May I keep this?"

"Sure. Why not? Your need is greater than mine. But if you do find her, tell her Fred Kline says hello."

Tom nodded. "Sure, I will. Fred Kline."

"Right." The man walked with him to the doorway. "Good luck."

"Thank you." Tom carefully rolled up the drawing. "Thanks a lot."

The man stopped him halfway down the stairs. "Tell her one more thing, will you?"

Tom looked back.

"Tell her I still love her."

Back in the city Tom bought a bunch of violets from an old woman on a corner and walked up to Newbury Street. Alice Blake wasn't in the gallery.

"She's out appraising a collection," the girl told him. Her eye shadow was purple today. She glanced at his violets and grinned. "That good, huh?"

"Could you see that she gets these?"

"Sure." The girl took the bouquet and sniffed it. "Nice. She *loves* flowers. I'll put them in water on her desk right now. Will she know they're from you?"

Tom shrugged. He wondered if he was imagining the tone of mockery in her voice.

"Well, not to worry," the girl told him. "I'll leave her a note."

He nodded and started out the door.

"Bye-bye," the girl called after him.

He hurried through the slanting sunlight toward the Public Gardens, disappointed that he hadn't been able to show Alice the drawing of Sylvia he had found. And disappointed because she hadn't been there to take the violets personally? Because he wanted to see her again?

"Be cool," he whispered to himself. It sounded like an empty incantation; it was no help at all.

90

The El Shibar Steak Pit had a narrow front of red glass, a big flashing sign. Tom smelled the steaks a block away. Inside, only two booths were occupied. An indifferent waiter in a dirty jacket showed him to a grimy, plastic-topped table and handed him a menu. Tom pried it open and studied his choices.

When the waiter came back with a glass of water, Tom ordered pork shish kebab and rice. The waiter raised one eyebrow but said nothing. He scribbled on his pad. "Something to drink?"

"A beer. Schlitz." Tom tried to look casual. All they could say was no.

The waiter was gone without another word. The beer came first and Tom sipped it slowly, discreetly studying the other diners. A man in a gray business suit, his belly hanging out over his belt, sat in a back booth reading a newspaper. A drink rested unnoticed on the table in front of him. He looked up and nodded when another beefy man joined him. The second man wore a shoulder holster. Tom wondered if they were plainclothes cops. He started to slide his beer out of sight behind the napkin holder.

"They won't shoot you," the waiter said from behind him. The plate of pork shish kebab and rice was dropped on the table. "Anything else?"

Tom looked up at him. His eyes had a vacant, unfocused look. "Is Paul St. Croix in the kitchen?"

The waiter shrugged.

"Could you tell him I'm out here?"

"Why?"

"I'd just like it if you did."

The waiter went away muttering, but a few minutes later Tom heard someone hissing at him. Looking toward the kitchen, he saw Paul leaning halfway through the swinging doors, grinning at him. Before Tom could wave, someone pulled Paul back inside the kitchen.

Tom left a big tip, bigger than he could really afford. His waiter nodded to him when he went out.

Back in his room Tom tried to read, but the book he had started didn't hold his attention. The light was dim, hard on his eyes. He would have to sneak in a larger bulb, despite the sign by the door that said:

USE OF LIGHT BULBS OVER 40 WATTS
FORBIDDEN IN THIS ROOM.

He lay on his side and looked out the window into the dark courtyard. Listening to the night sounds of the city, he fell asleep, and woke up with a stiff neck just before midnight.

He got up and went for a walk. The Public Gardens smelled of flowers. He sat on a bench and looked up at the glowing buildings. After a couple of minutes he shifted to a bench nearer a street light and took out Aunt Belle's letter.

He read it again slowly, from the beginning. The parts about his father he read twice:. . . . *I never much liked your father. . . . kept his children in rags in a shack in the scrub woods. . . . He was a bully. . . .*

Tom took out his notebook and found a fresh page. He stared at its empty surface for a long time and then he wrote:

Did I love my father?
I wish I knew.

Laughter came from the direction of the Common, insane cackling that sent shivers down his spine. He closed his notebook, replaced it in his pocket and walked back to his room.

92

Chapter Eleven

HE MISSED ALICE BLAKE at her gallery the next three times he dropped by. He did not see her again until Saturday afternoon and by then he had visited every gallery on his list, turning up no new leads.

She made him sit down in the stuffed chair. She leaned out her office door. "Amanda, see that we're not disturbed. Unless you get a real prospect, and I mean *real*." She closed the door and turned to look at him, a twist of a smile on her lips. "You seem to have had some sort of bizarre effect on that girl."

Tom shrugged. "I didn't intend to."

Alice laughed. "I'm sure you didn't." She sat down at her desk and held up a stoneware vase with his violets in it. "Aren't they pretty? A secret admirer came by with them the other day while I was out."

"Without leaving his name?" Tom wondered if the girl had double-crossed him and not told Alice that the flowers were from him.

"Well, Amanda did leave me some sort of note." Alice pushed through the papers on her desk. "Here it is. Hmmm. All she said was that I'd know who it was. Oh, and that he left his tricycle double parked."

Tom felt his neck burning. "She's a shit."

Alice's eyes danced with amusement as she looked at him. "She can be. But I think this," and she dropped the note into her wastebasket, "is more a dig at me than at you. I think she rather fancies you."

"I don't fancy her."

"The violets are beautiful," Alice said, her voice falling lower. "It was sweet of you to bring them by."

"I had a nice time Wednesday night."

Alice nodded. "Well, I have news, but first fill me in on what you've been up to."

He unrolled the drawing of Sylvia and showed it to her. "Is this Sylvia?"

Alice took the drawing and studied it, nodding her head. "Yes, it is. Where did you get it?"

"At a gallery in Brookline. Some guy there had kept it for years. He had a crush on her."

"She did have a rather disturbing impact on men. It was more than her looks. It was her air of vulnerability, no, let's say self-destructiveness. She was one of the walking wounded. Men wanted to rush out and do battle with her dragons." Alice handed the drawing back to him. "It's a good likeness. Do you recognize her?"

"Sometimes when I look at it real hard I see the girl I remember."

"But she's changed?"

"Yeah. It's not just the hair. She's . . . different now."

"But it's your sister?"

"I think so." Tom rolled up the drawing. "I know it is."

Alice stood up. "Would you like some coffee?"

Tom nodded and waited while she went out into the gallery. When she came back, she had a full cup in each hand.

"Cream, one sugar, right?"

"Yeah, how'd you . . ."

"I notice things. I watched you Wednesday night."

Tom sipped from his cup. The coffee was hot, strong. "What's your news?"

Alice opened her hands. "Maybe it's good. Hal, my friend on the police force, hasn't turned up any trace of your sister at the hospitals he's checked."

"Has he checked them all?"

"Some of the private clinics don't give out information, even to persuasive policeman. It would take a court order to pry even minimal records out of some of them." Alice shrugged. "Which is as it should be, I guess."

"But . . ."

"But Hal's very good. If he says he found nothing, then it's probably a dead end. Is that bad?"

Tom shook his head. "I guess I'm relieved."

"But we're back at square one."

"Not really. I have a picture of her now. I'm going to have some copies made."

"And?"

"And start visiting art supply stores. If she's still painting, she has to buy her oils and other materials somewhere."

"Seems logical, Sherlock."

He took out his notebook and flipped to the page where he had written:

Possible leads:
1. Rest of galleries
2. Alice's friend checking hospitals/institutions
3. Copies of drawing; check art supply shops

He crossed out items one and two. Across the top of this page he had written SYLVIA MACY, just as he had written it on most of the other pages in the notebook, hoping to fill them all with possibilities. He saw the name suddenly in a new way.

"I feel like an idiot!"

She looked at him over her coffee cup. "Why?"

"Her name is Sylvia Macy. Macy, not Stevens. She must have married someone. It's so obvious, I completely missed it."

"She was single when I was showing her stuff here."

"Yeah, but maybe she's divorced." Tom felt new excitement in the pit of his stomach. "Maybe there's an ex-husband around somewhere who might know where she is."

"And maybe she just changed her name after she left you with your aunt and uncle."

"Maybe." Tom shook away her doubts. "It's worth checking, isn't it?"

"More work for my friend?"

"Could you ask him?"

Alice scribbled in her appointment book. "Of course."

There was a knock on the office door.

"Yes?"

Amanda opened the door and looked in. "Mr. Flores is here."

"Thank you." Alice stood up as Amanda disappeared, leaving the door open. "Sorry, Tommy. Business calls." She leaned closer and whispered. "Very rich, very, very distinguished, lousy taste."

"Would you like to go to dinner tonight?" Tom blurted.

She took his hand in both of hers. "Oh Tommy, I wish I could, but I have an old friend coming into town tonight and he's crazy for some good seafood."

"Then tomorrow?"

Alice shook her head. "I'll be busy the rest of the weekend." At the office door she was still holding his hand. She squeezed it and kissed his cheek. "Thank you for asking me."

He shrugged, hoping his disappointment wasn't showing.

"No, really, Tommy. I hope you'll ask me again. Maybe next week."

He nodded. Out in the gallery, a tall, white-haired man with Latin features was standing by one wall of paintings talking with Amanda. Alice rushed over to him, holding out both her hands.

"Tony!" she cried. "How nice to see you today!"

The man kissed her on the mouth. Tom realized he was staring and looked away. He mumbled good-by and hurried toward the street door. Amanda got there before him. He swerved to avoid her as she began dusting a group of sculpted figurines.

"She hustles all the customers that way," Amanda told him. "You'd be surprised how it moves the duller stuff."

He glared at her.

"Boy, have you got a case," Amanda said and turned her back on him.

"Good luck, Tommy," Alice's voice followed him out the

door. He turned to wave to her but she was already in earnest conversation with her tall, rich, distinguished customer, Mr. Flores.

He called Aunt Belle and Uncle Carl Saturday night. It only made him feel more alone, although he took care to hide his down mood from them. He stressed the leads he had: the drawing of Sylvia, the two dozen photocopies he now had on his bed table back in his room, the business of Sylvia's last name that a police contact was going to check out for him. He made it sound as if finding Sylvia was a matter of another day or two. . . .

Only after hanging up, standing in the smelly telephone booth, gazing through the dirty glass at the street outside, did he admit to himself how he really felt. He bought a sandwich and went back to his room.

That night he dreamed he was walking across a long stone causeway with water on both sides, toward a field of grass bending under the sea wind, toward an island that always seemed to stay the same distance from him. Sheep grazed in the field, more sheep on the hills beyond the field. The wind was whipping up heavy seas; waves broke against the causeway. The granite block he was walking on began to crumble. . . .

He sat up with a cry, staring into the darkness of his room. Gradually the street sounds from outside filtered into his hearing as the dream faded. And then the name *Shepherd Island* went off in his head like the single note of a bell: the causeway ran from the mainland to Shepherd Island.

For the rest of the night he tossed about half asleep, half awake. In the gray morning he dozed, woke to church bells in the Sunday sunlight. He did not get up until someone knocked on his door.

"Who is it?" he asked, reaching for his jeans.

"Wayne."

Tom pulled on his pants, stumbled to the door half in, half out of them, opened the door to see his friend standing there.

"Hey Tom," Wayne growled at him. "You got those jeans on backwards."

Tom looked down. "Yeah, I do."

"Can I come in?"

"Jesus, will you just get in here and never mind being so damned formal?"

Wayne closed the door behind him while Tom put his pants on right. "Well, you're the one who moved to Boston," Wayne said. "How did I know you wanted to see me anymore?"

"You're here, aren't you? Will you knock off the bullshit? How'd you get here anyway?"

"Hitched." Wayne glanced around the room. "By the way, it's after twelve."

"Yeah, I was kind of beat. But how did you know where to find me?"

"Wasn't with the address you forgot to put in your letter."

"Yeah, I'm . . ."

"I wormed it out of your aunt. Suppose you tell me what's going on." Wayne walked over to the wall nearest the bed and looked at the drawing of Sylvia, the original, that Tom had tacked up there after having the copies made. "Who's this?"

"My sister Sylvia."

"You mentioned a sister in your note."

Tom pulled on his shirt. "Tell you all about it over breakfast." His dream of Shepherd Island drifted toward the back of his mind. "Let's go."

"You're on," Wayne said. "I'm starved." He followed

Tom out the door. "Can you really buy breakfast this late in Boston?"

Tom laughed. "They have places here you can buy breakfast at five in the afternoon."

They found a restaurant called Pewter Pot and ate their way through several orders of hot cakes. They finished with a third cup of coffee. Tom felt the caffeine setting his nerves on edge.

"That's an incredible story," Wayne said. "I mean, one day you're Tom Stevens—the Tom Stevens I've known since first grade—then you're Tom Stevens somebody else, with a sister and another home and . . ."

Tom nodded. "But I always had those pictures in my head to tell me I was different, except I never understood what they were."

"And you never told anyone?"

"I was afraid to. I really thought I might be crazy. Other people never talked about having pictures like mine in their heads."

"Think you'll find her?"

"I don't know." Tom shook his head. "Yes, I do. I'll stay here till I find her."

"What about school?"

"I've got more than a month of summer left."

"What about money?"

Tom shrugged. "I'm not broke yet."

Wayne picked up the check the waitress had dropped on the table between them. "Suppose I use that ten dollars you sent me to take care of this."

Tom started to protest, but Wayne ignored him. Outside the restaurant, they stood blinking in the glare of sunlight on the street.

"Show me Boston," Wayne said. "I'm just your country cousin now."

They spent the day exploring: places Tom had discovered during the week, places he hadn't had time for while hunting for Sylvia. They rode up to the observation deck in the Prudential building, took a ride on a swan boat in the Public Gardens, traveled the subways, walked through Quincy Markets. All afternoon Tom was haunted by echoes of his dream: the crumbling causeway leading to Shepherd Island. It had looked so real in his dream; had he been there as a boy?

Wayne noticed his distance and commented on it several times. On each occasion, Tom shrugged away his remarks. How could he tell his best friend that he felt separated from him? How could he tell him that there was a gulf now between them, a gulf widening with each passing day?

It was Wayne who named it. "You've changed," he said late in the day.

"No I haven't," Tom protested.

"Yes, you have. It's like . . ." Wayne looked around the street they were following toward Chinatown. "It's like you're somewhere else, not here with me."

To Tom, Wayne's words sounded like an indictment. Wayne had come all this way to see him and despite their spending the day together, Tom knew that somehow he had cheated Wayne, had denied him access to the inside of his new world. Their sightseeing had really been meant to cover this up.

Tom looked at him. "I'm sorry."

"Hey, don't apologize. I know you're going through a rough time."

Tom wanted to say more, but he couldn't find the right words. "Let's go pig-out on Chinese food," he said instead.

Later, Tom walked with Wayne to the highway by the river. "It's going to be a long hitch home," he said.

Wayne shrugged. "Be okay."

"You should have started back sooner, before it got dark."

"I wanted to spend the whole day with you."

At the edge of Storrow Drive, Wayne stopped and studied him. "You haven't told me the most important thing."

"What?"

"How're the girls?"

Surprised, Tom couldn't think of an answer. Finally Wayne stuck out his hand. "Forget it. It's not really important."

They shook hands. Tom watched Wayne cross the overhead walkway and go down the stairs on the other side two at a time. Wayne began walking slowly away, his thumb out to the passing cars. Tom watched as long as he could, then shouted good-by and hurried back into the city. He knew the gulf between them was real and maybe now uncrossable. For if it had not been so wide, he would have found some way to tell Wayne about Alice Blake.

Chapter Twelve

ON MONDAY Tom began visiting stores selling art supplies. Armed with his copies of the drawing, he went from shop to shop, asking questions, showing the picture, leaving it with his address on back whenever he could persuade someone to take it. There were dozens of stores that either sold artist's supplies or had departments that did; he would be days getting around to them all.

Playing detective was mainly hard work, he decided as he trudged around the city. Tuesday it rained. As he ducked through the showers, he kept telling himself that the next place he visited might be the one where Sylvia bought her paints. She was his one link to his past; without her he was lost in this gray middle ground, this limbo between one life and another.

Late Tuesday afternoon the rain stopped, but low, dirty clouds continued to swirl above the city. He rode the subway to Cambridge and walked through Harvard Square to a shop on a little side street that took him an hour to find. The evening air was chill, smelling of rain and smoke. His feet were wet; this would be his last stop for the day.

Inside the shop he breathed in the rich smell of paints, chalks, linseed oil, exotic papers, pencils. The only clerk still on duty was waiting on a manish looking woman dressed in a dirty nylon windbreaker. They were arguing over a bill the woman insisted she had paid. Her voice was gruff and low. As Tom waited and watched, she took out a pack of little cigars and lit one with a gold lighter.

"Carlotta, I'd really rather you didn't smoke in here," the clerk complained. He was thin and small, half the size of the large woman across the counter from him, and he seemed intimidated by her.

She blew smoke in his face and tapped the bill with one paint-stained finger. "You tell Gus to straighten out his bookkeeping. And don't send me another copy of this goddamn bill."

The clerk continued to squirm under her gaze. "I'll tell him, Carlotta, but why don't you drop by . . ."

"Has that special glue I ordered come in yet?" she interrupted him.

"I'll see."

While the clerk was gone, the woman wandered about the store. Twice she passed close to where Tom was standing. Both times she stared at him with frank, appraising eyes, as if she were doing something in her mind to his face, something brutal and uncomfortable. Her masculine features were accented by heavy, dark eyebrows and a trace of a mustache. A cloud of cigar smoke trailed behind her.

"Idiot!" she said once, nodding toward the back of the store.

The clerk came back with a gallon can. The woman took it from him and leaned it against the counter to read the information on its label.

"Can I help you?" the clerk asked Tom.

Tom showed him a copy of the drawing. "I'm looking for my sister. She's an artist named Sylvia Macy. Does she ever come in here to buy materials?"

The clerk studied the drawing, finally shook his head. "She might have been in here but I don't recognize her. She's not one of our regular customers."

Tom was too numb by now to feel much disappointment at each dead end he ran into. He wrote his name and address on the back of the drawing. "Would you mind holding onto this awhile, in case she comes in?"

The clerk shrugged. "Sure, but it will probably get lost in a day or two."

"Yes, just like my check!" the woman the clerk had called Carlotta said emphatically. She stared at Tom. "They lose everything here."

Tom nodded and thanked the clerk. As he started toward the door to the street, he heard the woman tell the clerk to add the gallon of glue to her bill. She followed Tom out onto the sidewalk. An early darkness was settling onto the city under the clouds. Tom began to shiver in his wet clothes.

"You are looking for Sylvia Macy?" the woman asked him. She fell in beside him as he walked toward the corner. "She is your sister?"

Tom nodded. "Do you know her?" The barest flicker of hope stirred inside him.

"I have heard of her. She is an excellent painter. There is an interesting element of primitivism in her work."

Tom felt the flicker of hope die.

"Have you been looking for her long?"

"A few days."

At the corner the woman turned away to the left. "Good luck. I hope you find her."

"Thanks."

"Wait."

Tom turned toward her. She was standing in the shadow of a dripping tree. He could no longer see her face.

"What is your name?"

"Tom Stevens."

"Tom Stevens," the woman repeated. "If I run into your sister, I will tell her you are looking for her."

The chill drove him into a small German restaurant for supper. It was night by the time he came out on the street again and headed toward the subway station in Harvard Square.

On the narrow, curving streets he soon got turned around. He realized his mistake only when he saw the river up ahead, the arch of a bridge. He took out his map and reoriented himself under a street light. Two blocks later he heard footsteps behind him and looking back, saw three boys following him.

"Hey, college boy, wait up," one of them shouted.

He debated making a run for it, decided it was too late.

"What do you want?" he asked, hoping to bluff his way out of this by adopting a bored, casual tone of voice.

"We see you're lost, we want to help," the largest of the boys said. He stopped a foot away from Tom, the other two boys crowding in on either side. Tom had only a dim impression of their faces: sunglasses over their eyes, broken teeth, short hair. One of them smelled of beer; his shirt had a dark stain. He drank from a can, then passed it to his friends.

"When a college boy gets lost, me and my buddies like to help out, that's all."

His friends laughed.

"I'm not in college," Tom said.

"He sure looks like one of them Harvard fairies to me," the boy on his left said.

"Let's show him the way back to school," the tall one said. He began pushing Tom toward an alleyway between two apartment buildings. Tom realized now that talk wasn't going to save him. He leaned to the right and drove his fist as hard as he could into the tall boy's face. He felt his knuckles slide into teeth, come away wet. During the second of stunned surprise he made his break.

They were after him a moment later. He had only a short lead on them. Ducking through a side street, he fell against some garbage cans, barely eluded his pursuers as he scrambled onto his feet again. As he ran he heard their heavy breathing behind him, their obscene snarls at his heels. He cut through a backyard, vaulted a low wire fence, darted between two parked cars, saw the van too late.

The van skidded when the driver saw him. Tom tried to spin away toward the far sidewalk. The van brushed his leg and sent him sprawling.

He was up again the moment he hit the pavement, only dimly aware of the burning pain along one arm and the hobbling ache in his leg. The driver yelled at him; the three boys were momentarily cut off. Tom used this confusion to cover his escape.

He ran on, street after street, until he was sure he had lost them. His arm was bleeding where he had skinned it in his fall. The muscles in his leg had cramped; he couldn't tell if there was more than a bruise where the van had hit him. There was a cut on his forehead. He sat down on a bench at a bus stop and waited there until he could catch his breath and stop trembling. Feeling something warm, he looked down and saw blood running from the knuckles of his right hand. He examined the cuts. He hoped he had done as much damage to the boy's face.

He asked directions back to Harvard Square. He lost himself in the crowds there, found the subway stairs and descended into the smells and shadows under the streets.

Riding across the bridge into Boston, he saw the lights momentarily above the river. He felt he was beginning to understand this city.

Last week at the restaurant called Rainbow's End he had glimpsed the view from the top. There with Alice Blake, he had tasted luxury and enjoyed a sense of how life should be.

But on Turnbull Street, in the room he rented from his landlady Mrs. McDougle, in the bathroom he shared with Paul St. Croix and all the other tenants on the second floor, in the greasy dining room of the El Shibar Steak Pit, most of all tonight in the back streets of Cambridge, he was seeing something altogether different.

Wednesday morning it hit him how close a call he'd had the night before. He woke up stiff and sore, scabbed and bruised all over. The leg that had taken most of the force when the van hit him was turning a livid purple. He put on his last pair of clean jeans and went around the corner to a laundromat. He had time there to assess his adventure, to gauge how close he had come to serious trouble.

He was still carrying all his money in his wallet. When his clothes were dry, he carried them back to his room. Before going out again, he took half his remaining cash and hid it in his closet.

He spent the day making the rounds of the remaining art supply shops. He was getting dangerously close to the bottom of the barrel. What would his next move be? Was there something else he was overlooking, some other possibility lying right before his eyes?

He had not seen Alice Blake since Saturday afternoon. He wondered if her friend on the police force had located Sylvia's ex-husband. If there was an ex-husband. It was just as logical to assume that Sylvia had changed her name after dumping him at Aunt Belle and Uncle Carl's house, in order to leave no trail behind her.

Why had she left him? Why had she run off and left him standing there crying on the porch? What had she feared so much that she couldn't stay?

He skipped lunch, ate two oranges during the afternoon instead. All he had so far was questions, questions at the art supply shops, questions in his head, questions without answers. He would settle for one solid fact, any fact at all, if it could just be sure and certain.

By evening he had exhausted his list of shops to visit. He went back to his room without stopping at Alice Blake's gallery on Newbury Street. He wanted to ask her again to have dinner with him, but his confidence was gone. He did not have the courage to risk another disappointment today.

He was barely into his room when someone began pounding on his door. He opened it to find Mrs. McDougle standing there, her hand a few inches from his face.

"Your room rent was due yesterday, Mr. Stevens."

"Sorry." He stepped back. "Come in."

"I'll just have my money, if you please."

He opened his wallet, counted out the bills, handed

them to her. As he waited for his receipt, he realized how angry he was.

"All I did was forget," he told her. "I wasn't trying to beat you out of your money."

"That's what they all say, Mr. Stevens." She waved the receipt at him. He had to catch it. "I have the most forgetful tenants in Boston."

As she left, he kicked the door shut after her. When another loud knock came almost immediately, he thought she had come back to hassle him about slamming the door. He pulled it open, ready to lash out at her. Instead, he saw Paul St. Croix.

"Say, friend. It's Wednesday."

Tom looked at the man's round, red face. "Yeah, I know it's Wednesday."

"My day off."

Tom remembered their conversation last week. "Right, Paul. We were going to talk."

Paul St. Croix looked at him. "I waited in my room."

"Sorry." Tom felt his anger at Mrs. McDougle melt away. "I just got here. Come in."

Paul St. Croix's work pants were so short that the cuffs pulled up onto his calves when he sat down in the chair by the open window. Tom saw that he wore no socks.

"You came to my restaurant," he said.

Tom nodded. "Yes, I did."

"Good food? Good food?"

"Yes, it was good."

"Who's that?" Paul was looking at the drawing of Sylvia Tom had tacked to the wall near his bed. "Who's that?"

"My sister Sylvia."

"I know her."

Tom looked at him. "No you don't, Paul," he said gently. "She . . ."

"I know her! I know her!" Paul stood up and walked to the wall and pounded the drawing with his hand. "I know her!"

"How can you?" Tom said. "You don't know her. You're mistaken."

Paul stared at him. Suddenly he headed for the door, talking to himself. Tom darted forward and stopped him.

"I'm sorry, Paul. Maybe you do know her." Tom kept his emotions locked up tight. He wasn't going to let himself get set up this easily for another disappointment. "Come on, sit down. I'm sorry."

With a wounded air, Paul pulled away from him and returned to the drawing. He pointed to it. "Nice lady," he said. "Real nice lady. Nice to me."

"Where did you know her, Paul?" Under the question Tom felt the first stir of excitement. He clamped down on it hard. "Where was this, Paul?"

"Where they put me."

"Where was that?"

"This . . . place." Paul looked uncomfortable. Tom wondered if he was lying, losing the threads.

"Tell me about this place they put you." Tom forced himself to sit down on the edge of the bed, very carefully, without any hope. "Tell me about it, Paul."

"I was having real trouble. I couldn't do nothing right." Paul began to wring his hands. His face was twitching with distress. "Everything was wrong!"

"It's okay, Paul," Tom said quickly. "That was then. That was long ago. Everything is okay now." He pointed at the wall between their rooms. "You have a job, a nice place to stay. Now is okay, Paul. But I need you to tell me about then, when you knew Sylvia."

Paul looked blank.

"The girl in the drawing there on the wall."

Paul nodded. "I called her Angel. She was my Angel." He stared at the drawing. "So pretty, so nice to me."

"Where was this, Paul?"

"I don't remember!"

"Was it some kind of hospital?"

"Maybe."

"Was she there too?"

Paul shook his head. "Not in my part. Another part."

"In another part of this hospital?"

"Maybe."

"Please tell me about her, Paul." The excitement wouldn't stay put any longer. He had to let it go; like a balloon, it flew quickly out of his reach. . . .

"Angel," Paul said. "She came to the sun room every day. She talked to me. Every day!" He glared at Tom.

"I believe you." Tom took a deep breath. "What did she talk about?"

"Me. She always said 'Paul, is today good' and I'd say 'Yes it is' or 'No it isn't', and then she would always have a little present for me. One time she gave me a picture of a flower. It was my favorite but they took it away from me. They . . ."

"Paul, did she ever talk about herself?"

Paul shook his head.

"Never?"

"She said 'Paul, is today good' and . . ."

"But sometimes she told you how she felt?"

"Maybe."

"Did she tell you where she lived?"

"She was in the hospital. Not where I was, in another part."

"I mean when she wasn't in the hospital. Where she lived outside."

Paul shook his head.

112

"Did anyone ever visit her?"

Paul looked at his feet.

"Did anyone ever come to see her?"

"I forget."

"Try."

"I can't anymore. I can't anymore! My head hurts!"

"It's okay," Tom said. "No more questions. But if you remember, will you tell me?"

There were tears rolling down Paul's round cheeks. He slowly nodded.

Tom stood up and put a hand on Paul's shoulder, leading him to the door. "I bet you like ice cream," he said.

Paul suddenly grinned. "I like ice cream. I love ice cream."

"Then let's go get some."

"Chocolate?"

"Sure, chocolate if you want."

They walked down the stairs together.

"Are you my friend?" Paul asked.

"Yes, I am."

"If I don't remember?"

Tom nodded. They walked out onto the front steps. "Even if you don't remember."

Chapter Thirteen

WHEN ALICE BLAKE came by Thursday night, Tom had fallen asleep in his clothes on top of the single blanket on his bed, after a day spent adrift in the city, trying to come up with a new idea, a new angle in his search for Sylvia.

It was the landlady, Mrs. McDougle, who woke him, rapping on his door to announce that he had a visitor downstairs. She went grumbling down the stairs ahead of him, brushed by Alice with a quick, suspicious look and clumped into her apartment, slamming the door behind her.

"Charming woman," Alice whispered. She was wearing designer jeans, a blouse with the top three buttons open, a sweater draped over her shoulders. A few drops of rain clung to her hair, catching the light from the dim bulb overhead. "I have the chariot double parked. Are you doing anything tonight?" Without waiting for his reply, she took his hand and pulled him out onto the steps. The wet pavements smelled of rain; thunder rumbled in the distance.

"I have great news," she told him.

"What?"

"It's a surprise."

The Fiat's top was down. They sped through the gleaming streets at the edge of a second shower. Alice ran three red lights to keep ahead of the rain.

"Why have you been avoiding me?" she shouted through the wind that rushed over them. "Were you pouting because I didn't accept your dinner invitation Saturday?"

"I wasn't pouting."

She looked at him and laughed. "I told you to ask me again." She reached over and touched his arm. "Don't be angry. Tell me what my favorite detective has been up to."

He told her about his fruitless circuit of all the art supply shops in the city.

"Bummer," she said. "No one recognized the drawing?"

"No. But the man in the room next to mine did." He quickly told her about Paul St. Croix. "Paul knew her in some place he was in, a hospital, I guess. She used to come into the sun room and talk to him every day. I don't know if I believe him or not." Tom hesitated, then plunged ahead. "Who am I fooling? If he can just remember more about it, he may give me a lead to where she is now."

"Are you going to ask him about it again?" Alice shifted gears as she spun the car around a slick corner.

"Yeah, I am. But he gets nervous and upset if you put much pressure on him. I have to give him a chance to remember on his own."

"Do you think he can?"

"I don't know." Tom looked around at the unfamiliar streets. "Where are we going?"

"My place." She looked up as the rain became heavier. "Almost there." She stepped down harder on the gas. "You could talk to his social worker."

"Who?"

"His social worker. He must have some agency looking after him. Maybe you could find out from them where Paul was. I could ask Hal to check their records for Sylvia's address."

Tom watched the streets flash by. "I'll talk to him again in a day or two. Maybe he'll remember more details. I hate to put pressure on him. And I don't want him to think I'm going to make trouble for him by going to whoever's in charge of him . . ."

"The social worker."

"Yeah. He's beginning to trust me. I don't want to blow that."

Alice touched his arm again. "You're a sweet kid, you know?"

"I'm not a kid."

Alice laughed. "Okay, grumps." She reached into the glove compartment and pushed the button on a small remote control device. Ahead of them a large garage door in the back of an apartment building began to lift. Without slowing down, she gunned the car through the doorway with only a couple of inches to spare and parked next to a white Cadillac.

On the elevator ride up she noticed the scrapes on his arm, the cut on his face. "What happened to you?"

"Nothing."

She stared at him until the elevator door opened on the tenth floor. "Maybe you shouldn't wander around alone at night," she said. "Or did that happen closer to home?" Before he could answer, she reached out for his right hand and looked at his scabbed knuckles. "Oh Tommy."

"It's nothing," he said, pulling back his hand. "I got hit by a car."

She gave him the twisted smile he'd noticed on her lips before. "And then you punched it."

He nodded.

She led the way along a carpeted hallway and opened the door to her apartment. He followed her inside. Soft music came from stereo speakers against one wall. Most of the opposite wall was taken up by glass doors that stood open onto a balcony.

"On a good day you can see for miles," she said. "Like twice a year at least." She dropped her sweater on a chair and disappeared into the kitchen. "Something to drink? Glass of wine, a Coke, beer?"

"A glass of wine."

She came back with a bottle and three glasses. She filled two of them, then dropped down on the plump couch and patted the cushion beside her. She handed him his glass, sat up straight so that she could make a toast.

"To not running into any more cars," she said. "Okay?"

He grinned and tapped her glass. "Okay."

They drank. He asked her about the other glass.

"Oh, that's for Penny when he gets here with your surprise."

"Penny?"

"That's just his nickname." She looked at him with a smile on her lips. "Are you disappointed that we're not going to be alone?"

He sniffed his wine, sipped it again. "I'm not disappointed."

She laughed so hard she had to put down her glass.

"Am I really all that funny?" he asked.

She bit her kunckle. "No, I'm sorry, Tommy."

He leaned back into the couch and looked around at the paintings on the walls. "Do you borrow these from the gallery or are they all yours?"

"Most of them are mine. I have a Photo-Realist canvas in the bedroom that would knock your socks off." She stood up suddenly and crossed the living room. "I'll be right back. If Penny comes, let him in, will you?"

"Okay."

While she was gone he wandered around the room, studying the paintings, touching a wood sculpture of a swan, so simple it was nearly abstract. At the balcony doors he looked out on the lights of the city. Rain slanted in on the wind. Lightning flashed behind a cloudbank in the rose-colored sky. He had never been in a room like this before. He felt hungry, as if he hadn't eaten in days.

"Aren't you at all curious?" she asked behind him.

He turned and saw that she had changed into a one piece lounging suit. The faded blue fabric appeared transparent but wasn't. "Curious over what?"

"Your surprise."

"I am, but you won't tell me."

"Not until Penny gets here."

They were halfway through the bottle when the buzzer rang and Alice hurried into the little front hall to unlock the door downstairs. When Penny came in, Tom stood up and waited to be introduced. He saw a tall, slender man, young but already balding, with a thin face, deep-set eyes, a quick, ready smile. They shook hands.

"Penny," Alice said, "this is Tom Stevens, Sylvia's brother."

Penny was wearing a stone pendant on a long gold chain. He fingered it absentmindedly as he studied Tom's face. "I think he looks like her," he said. "Don't you, Alice?"

"They have the same mouth. And look at his hands. Isn't that amazing?"

Penny took one of his hands before Tom could snatch it away. He nodded thoughtfully as he examined Tom's fingers.

"Do you know my sister?" Tom asked to cover his embarrassment.

"I did," Penny said. "When she was showing her work at Alice's gallery."

"But that's not the surprise," Alice said. "Show him, Penny."

Penny took a large manila envelope from under his arm and began to open it.

"Over here," Alice said. She switched on a light above a hardwood table.

"I'm a photographer, Tom," Penny told him. He took two enlarged black and white photographs out of the envelope. "I took these shots two weeks ago for a writer friend of mine who's doing an article on the revitalization of Boston. These," and he tapped the two photographs he had dropped onto the table, "were taken near Faneuil Hall. When Alice told me tonight about you and about your search for your sister, something went off in my head and I remembered that when I enlarged these pictures, I was surprised to . . ."

"Show him, Penny!"

Tom leaned closer over the photographs. Both were of a crowd watching a juggler perform. Penny pointed to a figure at the edge of the crowd. "Look here, Tom. I believe it's your sister. I'd swear it is."

119

Eagerly Tom picked up the first photograph and held it under the light. He saw a short, slender woman standing alone a few feet back from the rest of the crowd. Her face was clearly shown: her full mouth, her short hair, cut even shorter here than in the drawing, a sense of her wide open, overlarge eyes.

"It's Sylvia, I'll swear to it," Penny said again. "What do you think, Tom?"

"She looks like the drawing I have. But I remember her when I was little, when she was fifteen." He looked at them. "You two would know better than me. You knew her recently."

Alice took the photograph out of his hands and studied it. "It's her," she said at last. "Oh Tommy, it's her! It's too close a resemblance not to be. And you know what this means? She's still here, still here in Boston."

"At least as of two weeks ago," Penny added.

Tom picked up the second photograph. It showed nearly the same scene, except that in this one, the large bulk of a man stood beside his sister. There was something familiar about the man, but he couldn't pin it down. "Who's this with her?"

They both studied the photograph. "Can't tell," Penny said at last. "His face is turned away from the camera. He's talking to her, I guess."

Alice turned the photograph around three different ways. Finally she shrugged and dropped it onto the table. "I don't recognize him."

Penny replaced both photographs in the envelope, then handed the envelope to Tom. "Here you go. They're yours."

"I can keep them?"

Penny smiled. "Sure. I have the negatives." He squeezed Tom's shoulder. "Hope you find her. Really hope you do."

Tom thanked him. They sat down around the wine bottle and Alice poured Penny's glass full. She proposed a toast to success. They raised their glasses.

"Thank you, Penny," Tom said again. The wine and the excitement over the photographs were going to his head. "Up till now I was afraid to even think she might have moved away. I just kept . . ."

"She's here," Alice said, patting his arm. "Now we know she's here."

They drank the whole bottle of wine. Alice brought another from the kitchen. Tom clutched the envelope and tried to follow the conversation going on between Alice and Penny, but it became harder and harder to make any sense of what they were saying. He drank too much wine and then got up and found the bathroom where he was sick, covering up the noise of it by flushing the toilet three times. Back in the living room he fell asleep, their voices and the music in the background fading away like a dying wind. . . .

He woke up before dawn. He was still in the chair in which he had fallen asleep, but he was covered now by an afghan. His back and neck ached from the cramped position he had settled into while asleep. He looked around the dark room. The balcony doors were closed; he was alone in the living room. Light snoring came from the direction of the bedroom.

His head hurt. His mouth tasted like dry paper. Standing up, he tottered over to the hardwood table, found a pen and a piece of paper, scribbled a note:

> Sorry I passed out. Got too excited about the photos and drank too much wine. Really sorry. Thanks again.
>
> Tom

He hoped she would be able to read it; it appeared illegible to him in the faint glow of light from the kitchen. Retrieving his precious envelope containing Penny's two photographs, he tiptoed out into the hallway and let himself out.

The dawn streets were empty, beginning to dry now after last night's showers. He didn't have his map and it took him an hour to find a street he knew. The sun was just streaking the sky when he climbed up the front steps to his building. In his room he undressed with clumsy fingers and crawled into bed. Despite the long walk his head was still pounding, his stomach still queasy. The morning had an unreal quality; if he hadn't brought home the envelope, he might believe that last night was a dream.

He took out the two photographs and put on his light. He fell asleep studying the images of Sylvia standing at the edge of that crowd two weeks ago. His fingers gripped the photographs as if they were a lifeline: his one hard and certain fact, the one he had thought he would never find.

Chapter Fourteen

A WOMAN WAS YELLING in the courtyard below his window. He rolled over and looked at his clock: a quarter to twelve. He heard a slap, a child's high pitched crying.

A shaft of sunlight had found its way between the buildings to shine through one curtain on his window. As he watched, it faded. The child's crying dropped to a breathy whimper.

His head and stomach felt better, but his conscience didn't. He wondered what Alice and Penny had said about him when they realized he had passed out. He sat up to shake away the thought. When he did, the two photographs fell to the floor.

He picked them up and looked at them to make sure they were real. Then he carefully replaced them in their envelope and gathered his soap, washcloth and towel and went down the hall to the bathroom.

There was no hot water. That was all right, he thought. He didn't deserve any.

Downstairs, Mrs. McDougle looked up from her sweeping. "Late for work, aren't we, Mr. Stevens?"

He glared at her. "I don't have a job, Mrs. McDougle. What's more, I'm not even looking for one. But I pay you in advance for my room, so that's cool, right?"

His sudden attack took her by surprise. "All I care about, Mr. Stevens, is . . ."

"Is that you get your money. And you do." He skipped down the steps to the sidewalk, ignoring the sharp stab of his headache as it returned. He smiled back at her. "Actually, Mrs. McDougle, I'm independently wealthy. I just live here for the fun of it."

He stopped for coffee, pouring half of it into his water glass, refilling the cup with cream. When he reached the gallery, Alice Blake was talking with a man in a three-piece suit. Tom kept out of their way, drifting from the paintings on one wall to the pieces of sculpture in the back, waiting for her to finish.

Amanda bumped into him while he was staring at a bronze figure of a giant frog in the act of catching a bronze fly.

"She's been wondering where you've been hiding," the girl whispered.

"I know."

Amanda stared at him. "Playing hard to get?"

"No."

"It's sickening. Three times a day it's, 'Have you seen Tom? Did he come by while I was out? Are you sure he didn't at least walk by?' "

"Really?"

"Don't look so pleased with yourself. I just made that all up." Amanda curled her upper lip. "I wanted to see if you're gullible enough to swallow it. Which you are."

Tom looked at her closely. "You have two different shades of eye shadow on. Your left eye is a lot darker than your right."

She smiled coldly. "Bullshit."

There was a gilt-edged mirror above the bronze frog. He watched to see if she would glance at her reflection. When she did, he walked away.

"Turkey," she whispered to his back.

The man in the three-piece suit wrote out a check and agreed to take delivery of a large landscape next week. Alice walked with him to the street. When she came back, her cheeks were flushed with excitement.

"Oh I love to sell things," she cried, grabbing Tom's hands and squeezing them. "I should give myself the rest of the day off."

Amanda swooped by and plucked the check out of her fingers. She disappeared with it into the office.

Alice laughed. "She's never forgiven me for losing a sale last year when I misplaced a check and the client changed his mind instead of sending us a replacement. Sometimes I think I'm working for her, instead of the other way around."

When Amanda reappeared, Alice called to her, "Tom is going to help me pack up those Howell prints at my place this afternoon. You can reach me there if you need me."

Amanda nodded.

At the door, Alice looked back. "You can have Monday off. Fair enough?"

Outside she took Tom's arm as they walked around the block to where she had parked her car. "Do you think I cater to her too much?"

"Who?"

"Amanda. I keep meaning to be a real bitch to her, but whenever I look into those angry eyes of hers, I end up feeling sorry for her."

Tom shrugged his shoulders. "She stays with you, doesn't she?"

"Yes, but I think she only stays because she gets away with murder. If I come in late, she actually makes me feel guilty. In my own damn gallery!"

Tom laughed.

Alice stopped and looked at him in mock wonder. "Do that again."

"Do what?"

"Laugh. That's the first damn time you've laughed since I met you. I mean, really laughed." She ran one finger over his nose and lips. "You should do it more often."

At the car she handed him the keys. "Drive me home, Thomas."

He got in behind the wheel, reached across to open her door. The engine started with a satisfying rumble.

"Do you remember the way?" she asked.

"Not really. I wandered all over this morning finding my way back to my room."

"Serves you right for sneaking off that way. I was going to make you breakfast, creep."

"Sorry." His hand vibrated where it rested on the knob of the stick shift. "Did you find my note?"

She nodded. "You didn't have to apologize." She waved toward the street. "Come on, let's go. I'm starved. I always get ravenous after a big sale."

He drove out into a gap in the traffic. The shifting gave him trouble at first, but Alice looked the other way whenever he jolted the car from one gear into another.

"Now pay attention," she said. "This is your last chance to familiarize yourself with the route to my abode."

He smiled. "I could find it with my map, even if you didn't show me the way."

She laughed. "I bet you could."

Gradually the driving became easier. He took a corner almost as effortlessly as she did. She leaned against her door and watched him, a smile playing on her lips.

"Did you really feel that badly about drinking too much last night?"

He nodded.

"You shouldn't. You're young enough to get away with stuff like that. When I was in college I once passed out in the back of Jerry Nuburger's van. They thought I was dead, so they took me back to my dorm and left me on the lawn. Can you imagine?"

He laughed.

She patted his knee. "Good boy, Tommy. You're getting the hang of it now."

"What?" He glanced at the gear shift. "Driving this?"

"No. Laughing."

She made sandwiches and they ate lunch on the table beside the balcony doors. A strong sea breeze blew off the harbor. A wind chime on the balcony played constantly.

"It's nice here," Tom told her. "I really like it."

"I'm glad." She broke a carrot in half and gave him a piece. "Why didn't you wake me this morning when you decided you had to take off?"

"I didn't want to disturb you and . . ."

She looked at him. "Penny? Penny didn't stay with me."

He was surprised to see her face redden.

"I don't know what you think of me, but it so happens that I don't spend the night with every man who comes by to visit me."

"I'm sorry, I didn't . . ."

She slapped her hand on the table. "Will you stop apologizing for everything!"

"I'm not apologizing. I mean, I am but . . ." He glared at her. "It seemed a natural enough thing to imagine. He's an old friend of yours and . . ."

"He's gay."

Tom stopped. "I didn't know that."

"You should have. He liked you."

"Stop it."

Suddenly she laughed. "It's true. He thought you were cute as could be." She stopped when she saw the look on his face. She put her hand over his on the table. "Sometimes I forget how young you are. I shouldn't tease so much. Now it's my turn to say I'm sorry."

He looked at her. "Let's both stop apologizing for everything."

She nodded. "Good idea."

The telephone rang while they were drinking coffee. Alice went to answer it in the kitchen and when she came back a few minutes later she handed him a piece of paper. Then she stepped back, her face alive with excitement.

"Go ahead, read it."

"What is it?"

"Read it, will you!"

He looked down at the piece of paper and read what she had written there:

> William Macy
> 217 Lilac Drive
> Nihedic, Mass.

He read it twice. When he looked up at her again, his heart was beating quickly.

"Sylvia's ex-husband?"

"Yes, you were right. She was married, a long time ago,

and not for very long apparently. Hal really had to go digging. But there it is."

He folded up the piece of paper and placed it carefully in his wallet. "I'll call him, see if I can talk to him. Where's Nihedic?"

"West of Boston. At the edge of the suburbs. Real ritzy. I have some steady clients who live out there."

"Maybe I can go out to see him. He could be the . . ."

She reached over and placed her hand over his mouth. "Tomorrow. You promised to help me pack up those prints, remember?"

"Where are they?"

"In the bedroom. All the small framed ones, on the wall without any windows." She went to the kitchen and returned with a pile of newspapers. "Go ahead and start wrapping them. Be careful, they have glass over them. I'll go downstairs and scrounge up some boxes."

When she was gone, he went into her bedroom. Glass doors led from here onto the balcony also, and they were open to the sea breeze. A large potted palm rustled dryly beside the bed. One entire wall was covered by a huge painting of a couple embracing. It was so realistic, Tom had to walk within a foot of it before he could believe it was a painting.

"Oh, I see you've noticed Barbie and Ken," Alice said from the doorway. She dropped four boxes on the rug. "They're hard to ignore."

"It's . . ." He searched for the right word.

"It is, isn't it?" She joined him in front of the painting and nodded. "Photo-realism is so much more than realism. People used to think it was just a gimmick. I picked that up for a paltry sum. When I get tired of it, I'll turn it over for a nice profit."

She began pulling down the small framed prints from the other wall. He wrapped them in newspaper and together they wedged them into the cartons with more paper padding. It didn't take very long. Tom wondered why she had insisted he help her.

"We can carry them down to the car later," she said when they were done. "Another beer?"

He nodded.

When she came back, he was standing in front of the balcony doors, looking out. "There's a good view today," she said. "You can't take your eyes off it, can you?"

He turned and she handed him his bottle of beer. The funny little twisted smile was on her lips again.

"Tell me, Tommy," she said, "are you one of those arrogant youths who brags to his friends about his conquests?"

He started to shake his head. "No," he said, and then he found himself smiling, for no good reason, he thought. "I haven't had any conquests."

"Really?" She stared into his eyes. "We'll have to remedy that."

Chapter Fifteen

"IF YOU can arrive here before five o'clock," William Macy told him over the telephone Saturday morning, "I'll be able to see you. I have a dinner engagement tonight and after five will be impossible."

"I'll be there," Tom told him. He was surprised by William Macy's voice: middle-aged or older, certainly not young, richly modulated, cultured, a voice with a lifetime of money and the best schools behind it.

"Do you know the way out here?"

"I'll have to take a bus."

"Take the train from North Station. There are several that run out this way. I'm not far from the station here. You won't have any difficulty finding me."

"Then I'll see you in a couple of hours," Tom said.

"And you're really Sylvia's brother Tom?"

"Yes. Did she speak . . ."

"Come ahead. I'll be expecting you."

The line went dead. Tom took out his street map. He propped the door to the telephone booth open with his foot to let in some air. He found North Station on the map and plotted his route. As he was refolding the map, the phone rang. He looked at it for a couple of rings, then shrugged and answered.

Somebody wanted Tyler.

"This is a phone booth."

"I know that. See if Tyler's around, will you?"

Tom looked up and down the street. There wasn't anyone within a hundred yards. "Don't see him."

The person on the other end didn't respond. Tom repeated his negative report, but only the sound of breathing came over the line. Tom finally hung up.

When the telephone rang again as he was leaving the booth, he ignored it. The morning air felt like syrup. Two blocks from the phone he could still hear its insistent ringing.

The train ride out to Nihedic was a tour of tenement backyards and vacant lots until the city was left far behind. The suburbs then grew wealthier with each passing mile, until at the stop just before Nihedic; the countryside consisted of huge estates with lush, wide lawns, green and well-watered in the blazing, milk-white sunlight.

Nihedic itself was only a small village of two streets, with storefronts built to look like colonial houses. Tom was the only person to get off the train.

He stood for a moment alone on the station platform, squinting through the glare. The clock in a church tower at

132

the end of one street read a quarter to two. He decided not to waste time trying to find William Macy's house on foot, but walked instead toward the one taxi parked at the edge of the station parking lot. He looked at the address on the piece of paper Alice had given him.

"Two seventeen Lilac Drive," he said.

The driver pushed back his cap and nodded. As they left the village, Tom noticed the driver checking him out in his mirror.

"Hot enough day," the driver said.

"Yes," Tom agreed.

"Been hot all week. Need more rain, that's what we need."

Tom nodded.

"You a relative of Mr. Macy?"

Tom thought about it. "I was once."

The driver let him off in the circular driveway in front of a large brick house. The grounds, dotted with closely trimmed shrubs and edged with a row of flowering trees, stretched all the way down to a sluggish river covered with lily pads. He paid the driver and walked up the front steps. The door opened before he could ring the bell. A tall, white-haired man looked out at him.

"Ah, Mr. Stevens. You made good time."

Tom recognized the voice from the phone conversation. William Macy was older than he had guessed; he appeared to be in his late fifties or early sixties.

"You're surprised," William Macy said.

"I thought . . ."

"That your sister's ex-husband would be someone more nearly her own age? Perhaps it would have been better if I had been." He held the door open. "Come in."

Tom entered a long hallway. When the door shut behind

him, the noise echoed into a vast silence, as if the house were empty. He followed William Macy along corridors to a plant room at the back of the house. The air was cool here, with a breeze faintly smelling of the river drifting in through the screens. Somewhere out of sight a lawn mower droned: louder, softer, louder, softer. . . .

Above the stone fireplace at one end of the room Tom saw a portrait of himself. It looked down at him as if it had been awaiting his arrival.

"Remarkable likeness," William Macy said. "Especially when you consider she was working from memory, projecting how you would look years after she last saw you."

Tom walked slowly toward the painting. There was no doubt it was a painting of him. All the differences were meaningless next to the similarities: his hair, his mouth, his eyes. How could she know how he would look now, years later? What inspiration had driven her to paint this portrait despite the gap in time and space between them?

"It's all I have left of her," William Macy continued. "She painted it before we were married, while we were still happily playing in never-never land. She gave it to me as a wedding present." William Macy walked over to where Tom was standing beneath the painting and stretched one hand up toward it. "I insisted she allow me to keep it. The rest of the settlement went entirely her way. But I would not give up her portrait of you, Tom."

"Why?"

"She painted it with such love, with the love you can only feel for someone you've lost."

Tom looked at him, surprised by the emotion on the man's face. "You still love her."

William Macy smiled. "Of course I do. Who wouldn't?

So fierce, so fragile a woman, needing so much, taking so little." He paused as if to regain control of his voice. "I kept your portrait, Tom, because I can feel her love in it and that love is important to me."

They sat in wicker chairs beside a small bubbling fountain and sipped lemonade that a stout woman brought from the kitchen. William Macy gazed at Tom without hiding his interest. Tom brought out one of the photographs Penny had given him, unfolding it carefully.

"Is this Sylvia?" he asked.

William Macy's hands trembled slightly when he took the photograph from Tom. He studied it for a long time. "It looks like her," he said.

"But you're not sure?"

He shrugged. "It's not that good a picture. Where was it taken?"

"Near Faneuil Hall in Boston, two weeks ago."

"You're really determined to find her, aren't you?"

Tom nodded.

"Well, it could be her. Certainly could."

"And the man next to her?"

"What man?" He studied the photograph again. "Oh, I thought that was a woman." He handed the photograph back to Tom. "I have no idea who that is."

Tom refolded the photograph and returned it to his back pocket. The stout woman reappeared with a plate of cookies.

"Help yourself, Tom," William Macy said. He took two himself, then forgot to eat them. They slowly crumbled in his hands as he told Tom about Sylvia. The plant room seemed to grow dim as Tom listened, the light around them seemed to fade until all Tom saw was William Macy's lined face beneath his white hair.

"She was too volatile a person to be happy with me,"

William Macy told him. "Even there in Boston in the Beacon Hill apartment we picked out together, with a studio above it for her to work in. I think she was attracted to me initially because I represented steadiness to her, someone firmly planted on the ground, established. But these were the very qualities she came to hate in me."

The lawn mower in the distance stopped. Tom could hear birds now, singing in trees down by the river.

William Macy realized the two cookies in his hand had become mush. He dropped the crumbs into an ashtray, took out a clean handkerchief and meticulously wiped his fingers.

"Her moods would swing so, Tom, up and down, back and forth. She could be an affectionate little girl one day, wanting only to cuddle in my arms. The next day she would throw the name of her latest lover in my face." He looked sharply at Tom. "Don't misunderstand, I'm not criticizing her to you. If I had been the right man for her, perhaps she wouldn't have found it necessary to do the things she did. My friends warned me. I chose to ignore their advice."

He folded his hands on his knees.

"It just got worse, Tom. Finally, even I could see that although she couldn't bring herself to ask me for her freedom, she was dying, suffocating with me. After her suicide attempt . . ."

"She tried to kill herself?"

William Macy nodded. "You've got to understand the pressures she was under." He seemed afraid that Tom would judge his sister harshly. "The guilt that girl harbored in her heart . . ."

"Guilt over what?"

William Macy stared at him. "Why, Tom, leaving you, for one thing."

"There were other things?"

William Macy shrugged his shoulders and didn't reply.

"How did she try to kill herself?" Tom asked at last.

"An overdose of sleeping pills. She was with someone . . ." William Macy brought his handkerchief to his eyes. "I'm sorry, Tom. You have a right to know all I can tell you, but it's very hard for me. I manage now to go whole days without thinking of her."

Tom returned to his earlier question. "What else did she feel guilty about?"

"You mean you don't remember . . . you don't remember your childhood?"

Now the plant room was gone totally; Tom had stopped breathing. He looked past the man's tears, into William Macy's eyes. "I remember my sister as a girl with long, golden hair who sang lullabies to me and I remember the fields we played in, tall grass fields beside the sea. I remember her bringing me to my aunt and uncle in Delmory. Everything else is shadows. I know there's more. I just can't get hold of it."

William Macy sat up straight. His tears were gone. "Find her, Tom. She needs you. You need her."

"There's more."

William Macy glanced at his watch and stood up. "It's late. I have to get ready for my dinner engagement." He started toward the main part of the house. "I'll have Brad bring the car around and take you back to the station."

"There's more you could tell me," Tom repeated.

William Macy turned to face him. "Find your sister, Tom. I can't help you."

"And you don't have any idea where she is?"

William Macy shook his head. "Not the faintest, Tom. I don't even know if she's still alive."

"I have the photographs."

"If that's her."

"You said yourself it could be her."

"Yes, I did."

"But you don't really believe it." Tom struggled with his anger. "You don't believe it."

William Macy stared at him another moment, then turned on his heels and disappeared into the next room.

The chauffeur drove him to the station in a long black limousine. Tom felt lost inside it, was glad when he could climb out, thank the driver and find refuge on a bench beside the tracks. He had a long wait for the next train; he didn't get back into Boston until after dark.

He walked for hours before returning to his room. He needed to think, needed to sort out the things he had learned from William Macy. Most of all he had to find some way to understand Macy's reluctance to tell him all he knew about the past, the past Tom and Sylvia had shared as children.

Why had he brought their meeting to such a sudden halt? One moment he was sharing the most intimate details of his marriage, the next moment he abruptly dismissed Tom, all but threw him out of the house. . . .

Tom hardly saw the lights and bustle of the city around him. He walked within his own space, in a circle where no one, where nothing, could touch him.

Sylvia had tried to kill herself. William Macy said her feelings of guilt were enormous. He had implied, at least, there was more to this than the guilt she felt over abandoning Tom in Delmory. But what else was there? And why had William Macy sounded so shocked to learn that Tom didn't remember his childhood with Sylvia?

Tom began to run, through the streets that were only a blur of darkness and light, only a whisper of voices and laughter. He ran mindlessly, on and on, as if he hoped in some blind way to drive the shadows from his mind and let in understanding. . . .

He sank at last onto a bench and looking around, realized he was on the Common.

Where were the answers? Where was Sylvia? What terrible past had he come from, that when he finally found someone who knew, that person wouldn't tell him?

He walked toward Turnbull Street. It was midnight; he had wandered for hours and found nothing, no answers at all.

He climbed the stairs to his room, through the layered odors of the old, decaying building. When he turned the key and pushed into his room, he had no hint that anything was wrong until he switched on the overhead light. Then he saw the open closet door, the pulled out bureau drawers, and realized that his room had been ransacked.

It took but a moment to discover that his hidden money was gone.

He slammed the closet door, spun around on his heels to look at the disarray of his few possessions. Then he saw the drawing of Sylvia on the wall. Whoever had been here, whoever had taken his money, had also cut the drawing of Sylvia into shreds.

Chapter Sixteen

HE CALLED THE POLICE from the telephone booth outside the bar on the corner. When they finally arrived twenty minutes later in a patrol car that they parked halfway up on the sidewalk—its lights flashing luridly, its radio spitting out messages of other problems, other crimes—when they finally pounded on the street door and clumped up the stairs to the second floor, they had awakened the whole building and half the street.

"Why didn't you tell me first, why didn't you tell me first?" Mrs. McDougle complained as Tom explained to the two uniformed men what had happened. Beyond her puffy, sleepy face were the figures of other tenants peering in from the hallway.

"How much money was taken?" one of the policemen asked.

"One hundred and fifty dollars," Tom told him. He watched him write the figure down in a notebook.

"You kept it in the closet?" His tone implied that anywhere else would have been fine, but the closet had definitely been a dumb choice.

Tom nodded. The other policeman, taller, heavier, with a large sweat stain on the back of his shirt, was standing by the window.

"You always keep this window open?" he asked.

"Yes." Tom sidestepped Mrs. McDougle and joined him at the window. "It's too hot to keep it closed."

The sweating policeman nodded. "There's your problem." He pointed down into the dark courtyard. "Five-year old could break in here. Only thing would have made it easier would have been if you'd left a ladder out for him."

"You were gone all evening?" the first policeman asked him. He was still writing things down in his notebook.

Tom nodded. "I got back around midnight. I was gone just about all day."

"So the money could have disappeared this afternoon, even this morning?" He put away his notebook.

"Yes, it could have," Tom admitted. "I don't know that it was tonight."

Mrs. McDougle glared at him. "I keep a respectable building. God knows I try, despite the trash I have to rent rooms to."

Tom turned away from her and followed the first policeman to the closet. "You can't get my money back?"

The policeman shrugged. "I could tell you all kinds of things but . . ."

"But there's no chance."

For the first time the policeman looked at him long enough for their eyes to meet. "No chance. Petty stuff like this," and he waved his hand in a circle that seemed to take in the room, the building, the entire city outside, "happens so often, most of the time it doesn't even get reported. Someone spotted your open window, got in and out so fast he's probably spent the money already."

"It was most of the money I have left."

"Wish I could help you, son. Really do. But any promise I gave you would just be so much hot air."

His partner with the sweaty shirt joined them by the closet door. "Consider yourself lucky."

"Why?"

"You could have been sacked out in bed and gotten six inches of steel in your face if you woke up and surprised him."

The first policeman nodded. "People get snuffed around here for the price of a drink. I know you don't think so right now, but you are kind of lucky to get out of this with enough of your brains intact to figure on locking that window from now on." He slapped Tom on the shoulder.

"That's it?"

"We'll make our report," his sweaty partner said. "After that, it's in paper land."

Tom watched Mrs. McDougle go out into the hallway and begin yelling at the crowd of people gathered there. They ignored her except to shift positions when she blocked their view. Tom wondered where they had all come from; only two or three were people he'd ever seen before, passing in the hall or on the stairs. He looked back at the two policemen.

"Could it be someone who lives in this building?"

The first policeman rolled his eyes. "Christ, son, it could be anyone in the whole goddamn city!"

It was plain that they weren't really interested. Tom shrugged his shoulders, stared around at the disordered room. "The thief wasn't in such a hurry," he told them.

"How so?"

Tom nodded toward the tattered drawing of Sylvia on the wall near his bed. "He took time out to do that."

"Yeah, I noticed," the sweaty policeman said. "Who's the broad?"

Tom looked at him. "My sister." At the door to the hallway, he stopped them. "Why would someone do that? Cut up a picture that way? I mean, he got my money."

The first policeman shrugged. "Just a weirdo."

"Frustrated," the sweaty one said.

"Frustrated?"

"Sure. Nobody else around to cut up so he took it out on the picture of the broad. I mean your sister."

When they were gone, clumping down the stairs as loudly as they had climbed them earlier, Mrs. McDougle leaned in through his open doorway. "Next time there's trouble," she said, wagging a finger at him, "you let me know first, understand? No going off and calling in the lousy cops without you let *me* know first."

He nodded numbly, too tired to bother arguing with her. She was probably right. He had called the police and they had come and stirred up the whole building and accomplished nothing. When she was gone, he dropped into the one chair and spread his hands over his knees and sat there looking at his fingers, trying not to think about his bleak prospects.

But the money was gone, and what he had left in his wallet wasn't going to take him very far.

Back in Delmory, he still had half his bank account. But after that was gone, what then? Go home? Give up? He was no closer to finding Sylvia than when he started. All the leads he had turned up so painstakingly had led him nowhere. . . .

"Say, friend. Say, friend."

He looked up and saw Paul St. Croix standing in the doorway. "Hi, Paul," he said quietly.

"Trouble," Paul said. "Trouble, trouble, trouble."

Despite his gloomy mood, Tom had to smile. "You said it, Paul."

"All your money?" Paul asked.

"Most of it." Tom stood up and motioned Paul to come in. Then he closed the door.

"Angel!"

Paul had noticed the slashed drawing of Sylvia. Tom nodded. "A little extra touch to make it nicer."

Paul looked confused.

"I mean, it was a lousy thing to do."

Paul hurried out and came back a minute later with a roll of tape. Together they carefully repaired the drawing. Tears rolled down Paul's cheeks, splashing on the bed table where they worked.

"You really liked Angel, didn't you?"

Paul nodded vigorously.

"Well, she's practically good as new," Tom said, patting the taped drawing. "Practically . . ."

Paul suddenly grabbed his arm and shook him. "Ask me, ask me!"

Tom tried to calm him. "What, Paul? Ask you what?"

"Ask me, ask me!" He pointed to the drawing. "Ask me!"

"About my sister? About your Angel?"

Paul nodded. He closed his eyes very tightly, squeezing out the last of his tears. "Can I help you?"

Quickly Tom tried to collect his thoughts, tried to pick up the loose threads of the conversation he'd had with Paul on Wednesday, Paul's day off. . . .

"You know my sister," he said. "You know her as Angel."

Paul continued to bob his head. "I know Angel."

"Okay, Paul," Tom said, trying to calm his racing heart as much as steady Paul. "I'm trying to find her. I need you to remember if she ever told you where she lived when she wasn't in that hospital."

Paul shook his head. But then suddenly he said, "Cambridge."

"Cambridge? She told you she lived in Cambridge?"

Paul looked distressed. He covered his mouth with his hands. Tom gently pried them away.

"Who lived in Cambridge?"

"Friend. Angel's friend."

"Someone who visited her at the hospital?"

Paul nodded.

"Did you ever see this friend? This friend of Angel's who came to visit her in the hospital?"

"Man-woman."

"What do you mean, Paul? Did two people come to see her? A man and a woman?"

Paul swung his head heavily from side to side. "No. Man-woman."

The more excited Paul became, the harder it was for him to talk. Tom tried to soothe him, tried to slow him down. But he couldn't let this chance slip away.

"Not two people," Tom tried. "One man-woman?"

Paul nodded.

"I need a name, Paul. Did the man-woman have a name?"

Paul slapped his own head. Tom grabbed his arm to stop him for doing it again. "Don't Paul. Take time. You have the name somewhere. You can find it."

"Carl . . ." Paul said. "Carl . . . not Carl . . . Carl . . . not Carl . . ."

"A name like Carl?"

Paul nodded so hard beads of sweat danced off his forehead. "Carl . . . not Carl . . . Carl . . . not Carl . . ."

Inspiration moved Tom's lips: "Carlotta? Was the name Carlotta?"

"Yes!" Paul exploded. "Carl-lotta, Carl-lotta!"

"Carlotta from Cambridge?"

Paul nodded. "Carl-lotta from Cambridge! Carl-lotta from Cambridge!"

Tom quickly unfolded the photograph of Sylvia at the edge of the crowd near Faneuil Hall, the photograph in which a friend stood beside her, a friend he had mistaken for a man. . . .

"Is this her, Paul? Is this Carlotta here next to your Angel?"

Paul seized the photograph and brought it close to his face. "Carl-lotta," he said. But he was stroking Sylvia's face with his fingertips. Tom took his index finger and placed it on the shadowy figure beside Sylvia.

"Carlotta?" he asked.

"Yes," Paul said. "Yes, yes."

Tom put his arms around Paul and hugged him. Paul hugged him back. Over his shoulder Tom stared at the dark window that looked out on the courtyard, but in his mind he was seeing the art supply shop in Cambridge and the mannish-looking woman arguing with the store clerk about a bill she claimed she'd paid.

The clerk had called her Carlotta, and she was certainly big enough and masculine enough to be mistaken for a man, especially in a dark photograph. William Macy earlier today had looked at this same photograph and thought it was a woman standing next to Sylvia and had said so, and still Tom hadn't guessed.

But he had it now. All the pieces were falling into place.

146

The clerk in the art shop had called her Carlotta. She overheard Tom talking with the clerk about Sylvia, and she followed him out into the street and questioned him. At the time he'd thought little of it: she said she had heard of Sylvia, but so had a lot of other people. But now, looking back, he recognized the veiled intensity behind her questions.

Tom hugged Paul as hard as he could. "You did it, Paul. You gave me the key."

"Carl-lotta," Paul said again.

Tom nodded. "Carlotta is the key."

Tom could not sleep at all during the rest of that night. Early Sunday morning he took a chance and went out to call Alice Blake. He found one A. Blake in the telephone book and dialed the number. As he listened to it ring, he nearly lost his nerve, nearly hung up.

Yet Friday, wonderful Friday, was fresh in his mind. The memory of it ran on and on, over and over in his head like a song that wouldn't go away. . . .

He pulled the phone from his ear. It was too early in the morning, she was obviously asleep, she might be . . .

"Hello?" Her voice was low and far away. He jammed the receiver against his ear again. "Who's this?" she asked.

"Tom," he said, cleared his throat, said it again.

"Tom, my God, where are you? What time is it? Are you all right?"

"I'm fine. I'm in a phone booth."

"It's six-thirty in the morning. Don't you ever sleep?"

"Should I call back later? Sorry if I . . ."

"Don't be silly. I'm awake now. If you hang up, I'll kill you."

"I know where Sylvia is. I mean, I know who can tell me.

The person in the photograph, the person standing next to her, is a woman named Carlotta who's an artist in Cambridge."

"Never heard of her."

"Well, she buys materials at a shop near Harvard Square."

"How do you know all this? What makes you think she's the one in the photograph? It looked like a man to me."

"*She* looks like a man. I ran into her while I was going around to all the shops. She asked me a lot of questions. She . . ."

"Tom, you're not making any sense."

"I know. It's confusing, but I'm sure I'm right. You remember Paul St. Croix, the retarded man who lives in my building, who recognized the drawing of Sylvia?"

"Yes, I remember. You told me about him, but what does . . ."

"Well, I got ripped off last night and he came in to tell me he was sorry . . ."

"He robbed you?"

"No, no, he just came home and heard about it and . . ."

"Tom, for heaven's sake!"

"I'm trying, damn it!"

She laughed. "Maybe I'm still asleep."

"No, it's my fault. I'm trying to tell it all at once. All the pieces just fell into place and . . ."

"Come over," she said. "I'll feed you some breakfast and you can start at the beginning."

"You're sure?"

"Well, if you'd rather not see me when I'm half asleep and furious with some clown who calls me up before dawn to give me a line of gibberish that . . ." She took a deep breath. "Tom, would I ask you over if I didn't want you to come?"

"No."

"Then get your ass over here."

She hung up. He looked at the receiver and grinned. On the long walk to her apartment building, he found a bakery that was open and bought half a dozen doughnuts. He looked at a bouquet of silk daffodils in a vase on the counter.

"Could I buy one of these?" he asked.

The girl behind the counter handed him one with his change. "Be my guest," she said.

Alice met him at the door to her apartment. She was wearing a long, thin robe. The twisted smile was on her lips. She plucked the silk flower out of his fingers and kissed him.

"It's pretty," she said. "Thank you."

Over breakfast in her kitchen he told her about the robbery, about Paul's insistence that Tom ask him more questions about Sylvia, leading up to the revelation that Sylvia's visitor at the hospital had been a manish looking woman named Carlotta, from Cambridge, who happened to match exactly the appearance of a woman of the same name Tom had run into at the art supply shop near Harvard Square. As he filled in all the details, Alice nodded her head.

"Now that's beginning to make some sense," she said. "Why didn't you tell me that on the phone?"

"I did."

She smiled. "Dear Tommy, I wish I had a recording of what you *did* say. I'd play it back to you right now."

He bit into another doughnut. "I guess I was pretty excited."

149

"What's next?"

"Monday I go back to that shop in Cambridge and find out where this Carlotta lives. Then I go ask her why she didn't tell me she knows Sylvia personally."

Alice nodded. "Why do you suppose she didn't tell you?"

Tom shook his head. "I can't even guess. But she stood right next to me on the sidewalk and asked me all those questions about who I was looking for and who I was and pretended she had only heard of Sylvia as an artist. Told me something to the effect that . . ." Tom looked at the kitchen wall for a moment, remembering the exact words. "That Sylvia as a painter had *an interesting element of primitivism in her work*. And all along she knew where Sylvia was."

"At least we think she knows."

Tom put down his coffee cup. "She does. She was with Sylvia two weeks ago when Penny took those photographs."

Alice nodded. "It fits together."

"It does. And . . ."

Alice put her fingers to his mouth. "Enough, my sweet detective. It's Sunday. Even detectives get to take Sunday off."

He watched her get up from her chair. She came over to his side of the table and put her hands on his shoulders.

"Yes they do, Tom," she said. "During the entire day Sunday it's forbidden to do any detective work at all." She kissed his nose. "I have that from a reliable source."

"And we both know . . ." he said, losing track of the joke as he stared at her.

She smiled. "Yes. We both know how much detectives respect reliable sources."

In the evening he watched as light coming through the open balcony doors cast fading patterns on the opposite

150

wall. Far below and far away, the city rumbled quietly into the night. As he listened to the far off sounds of a million other people, he felt for the first time in his life as if he could reach out and touch time itself with his hands, touch it and hold it, whole within his grasp.

He wanted time to stop. Sylvia was out there somewhere among those million people, and he knew he was closer now to her than he had been in all the years since she had left him in Delmory. He could go on now and complete the search, find her, touch her, ask her why. . . . He was close enough now to sense success within his reach, yet he was afraid. If time stopped now, he would never know the truth. Did he really want to know the truth?

Night came while his eyes were closed, proving that time still flowed ahead, taking him with it. The decision, somehow, had been made without his real choice. He would continue to search for Sylvia, and the truth, finally, would be his to know. . . .

"Want to go out for supper?" Alice mumbled next to him.

He thought about it. "Yes, let's go out."

She sat up and looked down at him. He could barely see her in the dark, but she reached over and touched his face, felt his tears.

"Oh Tommy . . ."

"It's okay," he told her. "Let's go out. I know just the place.

"Where?"

"The El Shibar Steak Pit."

"Really?"

"Yeah, my treat."

"You're about broke, remember?"

"That's why it's the El Shibar or nothing at all."

She laughed. "Okay."

151

Part 3

CIRCLE HOME

Chapter Seventeen

THE CLERK in the art supply shop in Cambridge was not the same one who had been there last time, but he quickly recognized the person Tom was asking about.

"Sure, you mean Carlotta Sims. She buys a lot of her materials from us. She's really an amateur, but she has money enough to indulge herself."

"She's not a real artist?" Tom asked.

"Well, aren't we all, in one way or another," the clerk said. He folded his arms across his chest, covering the lettering on his sweatshirt. "She may even sell some of her work, but it's strictly self-indulgence, like her bohemian pose."

Tom looked at him.

"You know. The little cigars, the Army and Navy store

fashions, all that contrived garbage: the artist as basic slob. Gross chic, I call it." He laughed. "You follow what I'm saying?"

Tom nodded.

"But I shouldn't be so catty. She can be difficult to deal with but she does a lot of business with us." He now looked more closely at Tom. "What do you want with her?"

"I think she knows where my sister is. I'm looking for my sister."

"I see." The clerk continued to look at him appraisingly, as if to decide how true his explanation was. "Well," he said at last, "I'll give you her address." He moved toward the back of the store. "Just don't tell her we gave it to you, okay?

"Okay."

The clerk came back a moment later with the address, which he had written on a scrap of construction paper:

Carlotta Sims

Studio E

1011 Pell St.

"It's down toward Central Square," the clerk told him.

"I'll find it." Tom stuffed the piece of paper in his shirt pocket. "Thanks."

"No problem." He watched Tom walk to the door. "Who is your sister?" he asked. "Anyone I'd know?"

"Sylvia Macy."

"Really?"

"Yeah."

"That doesn't surprise me. Carlotta collects famous types. She's a pro at that. Why did your sister stop painting?"

"I don't know." Tom hurried out into the street. At the corner, looking back, he saw that the clerk was standing in the shop doorway watching him.

156

The morning sun was trying to break through the clouds by the time he located Pell Street. The air was heavy, oppressive. No wind stirred the leaves on the small trees that had recently been planted at the edge of the sidewalk.

The building at 1011 was newly renovated. The foyer still smelled of paint. Someone had left the inside door propped open. He climbed the stairs to the top floor and rapped on the door marked with a small brass E.

He had to knock for several minutes before Carlotta Sims opened the door a crack and looked out at him.

"What do you want?"

"I'm Tom Stevens," he said.

"That should mean something to me?"

"I'm looking for my sister Sylvia Macy. We talked last week."

A flicker of recognition might have crossed Carlotta Sims' face, but through the narrow opening, Tom couldn't be sure. "Why are you here?" she asked.

Tom tried to find a polite way to tell her he thought she had lied to him. During these silent moments she started to close her door.

"I think you know where Sylvia is," he said quickly.

"And why do you think that?"

Tom wished he had a clear view of Carlotta's face. "For one thing, I have a photograph of the two of you together."

"I find that hard to believe."

"Why won't you tell me where she is?"

"Because I do not know. Now if you will get the hell . . ."

She tried to shut the door. He forced his foot into the opening.

"Idiot!" she shouted. She kicked at his foot, hit his ankle instead. He winced but held his ground.

"I want to see Sylvia. You know where she is."

Suddenly she was waving the point of an umbrella in his

face. "Get away from here! I do not put up with street punks calling me a liar!"

He jerked his head to one side. The point of the umbrella, a lethal, silver blur, missed his eyes by an inch or two. In another moment she had brought it down hard onto his foot.

With a howl he jumped back into the hallway. The door slammed shut. "Get out!" she shouted from behind it.

Leaning against the wall, he picked up his foot and tried to massage away the pain. His sneaker had provided little protection. Tentatively, he put his weight on the foot and limped toward the stairs. He knew she was crouched behind her door listening for his steps. He had not counted on such formidable opposition.

As he went downstairs, his right foot twinged each time he put weight on it. For a moment he wondered if he was wrong about Carlotta. Maybe she didn't know Sylvia. Maybe he had the pieces put together incorrectly.

He shook his head angrily. No, he was right and she was lying. He didn't know why, but she was lying.

He stopped on the steps outside and looked up and down the street. On the other side and halfway to the corner, an alley was partially blocked by piles of cardboard cartons. He walked painfully around the block and through the alley from the other side. In a few minutes he had taken a position behind the cartons, out of sight of the windows of 1011, but with a good view of the front door. He would be able to see everyone who went in or out of the building.

He settled down to wait. His foot still throbbed but he forced himself to ignore it. If Carlotta was the key, and he was going to hold onto that idea until there was real proof that she wasn't, then he had to stick with her until she tipped her hand, stay close until, one way or another, she led him to Sylvia.

It had started to rain. The drops fell through the narrow opening above the alley, slowly, steadily dripping on his head, his shoulders, his back, gradually soaking through his shirt to the skin inside. The morning slipped slowly into afternoon. The clouds grew darker. His stomach growled constantly.

A window opened above his head. "What are you doing out there?" someone demanded in a thin, reedy voice.

Tom didn't look up. "Waiting for a friend."

"If you're not gone in ten minutes," the voice said, "I'm calling the cops."

He stayed put. He couldn't take the risk that looking out a window or starting out the door, Carlotta might spot him. His one chance lay in making her think he had given up.

The voice above his head threatened him with the police twice more as the afternoon passed. He couldn't tell if the voice belonged to a woman or a man. It grew angry toward evening.

"You're not waiting for a friend. You're up to something else. No good, I bet. I'm calling the cops this time if you don't get out of that alley."

He ignored the threat.

"At least say something," the voice demanded.

"Like what?"

"Tell me why you're there. You're getting soaked."

"I know."

"But why?"

Tom shrugged. Rain drops rolled down his forehead into his eyes.

"You kids are crazy these days," the voice said.

Tom heard the window close. Just before dusk it opened again.

"Still there! I don't believe this. You've been there for hours."

The rain had stopped. Tom watched lights come on in windows up and down the street. He still had a good view of Carlotta Sims' building. A street light at the corner bathed the doorway of 1011 in a harsh, blue-white glare.

Slowly, during the long, long wait, standing there behind the soaking cardboard cartons, he became obsessed with the thought that his sister was inside Carlotta Sims' studio. This was the reason Carlotta had opened her door just a crack, had driven him off with such violence. Sylvia was inside, and Carlotta didn't want her to know he was there at the door asking about her.

Why?

Any reason he could imagine seemed too wild to believe. But he had time to think of a hundred possibilities.

It was an insane theory; in some dry corner of his mind, he knew just how insane it was. But Carlotta *was* eccentric. And if something didn't happen soon, he would go crazy too. . . .

He almost didn't see her when she came out. He was fidgeting with a garbage can, trying to arrange a way to sit down. He looked over just in time to see Carlotta walking along the sidewalk toward the far corner. He recognized her dirty nylon windbreaker, the man's roll to her walk. He waited until she had turned the corner, then he hobbled out of the alley and crossed the street. Inside her building he climbed the stairs to the third floor and knocked on her door.

He knocked again. He rang the buzzer, which he discovered on the far side of the door. "Sylvia?" he called. "Are you in there?"

He began to pound the door with his fists. He realized he was losing control, that the long day in the rain, the pain in his foot, the hunger and the chill that filled his whole body now, had driven him a bit over the edge. He was angry, hurt, a little desperate now, driving himself into action after hours of standing there waiting. His knuckles began to bleed. Someone opened a door further down the hall.

"Are you looking for Carlotta?" a man with a heavy beard asked him.

Tom pulled his hands away from the door. "No," he said. He took a deep breath to stop the tremor in his voice. "No. I'm looking for Sylvia Macy."

The bearded man walked part of the way up the hall toward him. There was a white, plasterlike substance dusted over his beard. His overalls were covered with the same powder.

"Sylvia?" he said. "She flipped out about two weeks ago. They lugged her out of here in an ambulance. Nervous breakdown, I guess. Carlotta says she's had them before."

"Do you know where they took her?"

The man shook his head. Bits of the white powder fell from his beard. "I don't. But I'm sure Carlotta can tell you. She's gone to visit Sylvia three or four times."

Tom nodded. "I'll ask her." He backed toward the stairs.

"Carlotta must have just stepped out. She should be back soon."

"Okay." Tom stopped at the head of the stairs. "How long ago did you say Sylvia . . ."

"Popped her gourd?" The bearded man counted on his fingers. "Less than two weeks. Let's see, I delivered that piece to . . ." He looked up at Tom. "Ten days ago. A week ago last Friday."

A calm part of Tom's mind did the calculations: Penny's photograph showing Sylvia and Carlotta together outside Faneuil Hall had been taken two weeks ago last Thursday. So all the pieces still fit together: Sylvia's breakdown had occurred *after* Penny took the pictures. . . .

"Thank you," he told the bearded man.

"Glad to help."

Tom took the steps carefully, but the pain in his foot wasn't bothering him so much now.

He was closing in. Sylvia's trail was getting warm. He was only ten days behind her now, and Carlotta Sims was still the link, still his best hope of finding her.

Chapter Eighteen

TUESDAY MORNING at a little after eight Tom was back at his hiding place in the alley across the street from Carlotta Sims' building. Dry clothes and a sunny, warm morning made the waiting less of an ordeal, but still, by noon, he was restless, stiff, impatient for something to happen.

The voice from the window above his head hailed him just as distant bells struck twelve. With the voice came the pungent odor of something spicy cooking.

"I've been watching you," the voice said. "I've decided someone should break the news to you."

"What news?"

"Your friend isn't coming."

Tom chanced a quick look up. He saw a pinched, pale face, thin white hair, sharp eyes.

"He looks up at last!" the voice said. "He dares to show his face."

Tom looked quickly back at Carlotta's building. "Why do you keep talking to me?"

"It's against the law? You camp out in my alleyway and I should respect your right to privacy?"

Tom smiled. "It's a public alley."

"It's my alley," the voice corrected him.

"Okay."

"Are you spending the summer there?"

Tom shook his head. "I hope not."

"Is this a CETA job?"

"What?"

"Does the government pay you to stand there watching the street?"

"No, of course not."

"Just asking, just asking," the voice said.

The smells coming through the window above him grew stronger, more enticing.

"What are you cooking?" Tom asked.

"Chicken soup with barley. Why? You're hungry?"

"Yes."

"Well, come in and have a bowl."

"I can't."

"You'll miss something?"

"I might."

"Then wait." A few minutes later the voice was back at the window. "Look up."

Tom looked, and saw thin, white arms lowering a small plastic bucket down toward him on a string. He reached up and guided it down the last couple of feet. The bucket was half filled with soup, a spoon already in it.

"Eat hearty. When you're done, tie it back onto the string. That's a Tupperware bowl."

164

"Thanks."

"It's nothing. Maybe if you're waiting to mug some poor innocent victim, you'll think twice about it now. The milk of human kindness will flow a little in your veins, you'll hit gentle."

"I'm not waiting to mug anyone," Tom said through a mouthful of hot soup.

"So you say."

"This soup is great," Tom said a moment later, but the voice was gone from the window.

A few minutes later Carlotta Sims came out the front door of her building, stood on the steps for a moment looking carefully in both directions, then struck off up the street in long, quick strides, a black satchel swinging at her side. Tom quickly tied the soup bucket back onto the string, called another thank you to the empty window above his head and hurried after the rapidly disappearing, portly figure of Carlotta.

His right foot still twinged slightly from the bruise Carlotta had inflicted with the point of her umbrella yesterday. The pain forced him to limp slightly, but it did not slow him down.

He kept as far back as he dared: the way Carlotta had surveyed the street before leaving her front steps told him that she was at least thinking of the possibility of being followed. He was not wrong. At the corner she turned suddenly and looked back. Ready as he was for this sort of tactic, he still barely had time to step behind a parked delivery van.

His heart beat more quickly. If she feared he might be following her, then she could only be going to visit Sylvia. This was no ordinary trip to the market.

Keeping well back, he followed her all the way to Central

Square. He sensed that she would be extra careful here, and so he was buying a newspaper at a magazine stand with his back toward her when she paused at the top of the subway entrance. He kept track of her in the reflections in a storefront window. She looked all around before plunging down the stairs into the station. He dodged through the traffic and entered the stairway behind her. He saw her black satchel turn the corner of the corridor below.

He waited beside a map of the subway system until she had purchased her token and gone through the turnstile. When he joined her on the platform, he kept his distance, his face hidden behind the newspaper he had just bought a moment ago up on the street. The platform was crowded. He used the people as an extra screen.

Carlotta seemed confident. She leaned against a steel pillar and gazed off into space, as if now that she thought herself safely away from her street and undetected in the underground, she was off her guard, relaxed, no longer expecting to be followed. He would do nothing to change this.

When the train came, he guessed she might have a momentary return to watchfulness, and so he allowed her to enter her car first and did not step on until the last possible moment, and then through a different set of doors. He jockeyed his way through the crowd until he had a partial view of the black satchel she held at her side.

As the train made its stops at Kendall and Charles stations, he remained braced for a sudden exit. But the satchel stayed put. The odds favored her getting off at Park Street, if only to change lines. As the train squealed its way back into the tunnel, he edged closer to the doors. Even then, he almost lost her when she got off the train on the other side and climbed to the upper level on a different set of stairs.

During the minute or two that she was out of sight, he furiously raced up the stairs on his side, then searched through the crowds on the upper level. There was the danger that he could meet her head on. But he was more concerned that if he stayed cautiously in one place, she might leave the station unnoticed.

Yet, if he went to the stairs that led up onto Boston Common, he might lose her for good among the trolleys. It was a difficult moment, with no acceptable choice. He tried to cover all bases by edging toward the stairs while looking back at the crowd. When he spotted the satchel disappearing around the front of a trolley, he had to fight his way back through a surge of people intent on leaving the station. He raced toward her, found her, lost her, barely had time to squeeze his way onto the car he thought she had boarded.

He was wedged between two people on the steps, his back to the folding doors. The trolley made three stops before he managed to fight his way up off the steps. He had not seen her get off. If he hadn't made a fatal error back at Park Street, she should still be on this car.

Two stops later the crowd had thinned enough to permit him a glimpse of Carlotta in a seat toward the front of the car. Her back was toward him but he recognized her rough haircut. The black satchel sat under her arms in her lap. He took a deep breath and wiped the sweat from his forehead.

As the trolley emerged above ground, he realized he was in a part of the city he had never seen before. Streets widened, buildings flattened as the trolley left downtown Boston further and further behind. There were trees, small parks, neat and tidy neighborhoods hidden away on side streets.

When Carlotta got off alone, Tom didn't dare get off with her. He rode to the next stop two blocks away. As he hurried down the steps, leaving his newspaper behind on his seat, the driver shouted at him.

Tom turned. "What?"

The driver pointed toward the fare box. "Forty cents. You got to put in another forty cents."

Tom reached into his pocket, found only a quarter. He took out his wallet.

"I can't give you change," the driver told him in a bored voice.

Tom took out a dollar and jammed it into the fare box. He limped down the steps and ran back toward the corner where Carlotta had got off. The fare mix-up had cost him precious time, time he couldn't afford to lose after the extra two blocks he had already been forced to ride.

The wide avenue was less crowded than the streets in the middle of the city. People wandered along the sidewalks singly or in pairs. A group of summer students lounged on the grass in front of a college building. He looked around for Carlotta's large bulk. She should stand out plainly in such an open space, unless she had already taken a side street.

But which street? He couldn't come this far through such crowds to lose her here where he could see for blocks. He forced himself to think calmly. As the trolley had pulled away from her stop, he had seen her cross the street. He darted over, narrowly avoiding a speeding bus. He walked up the nearest side street. A young boy stood beside a bicycle adjusting a package in his basket.

"Did a large woman come by here?" Tom asked him. "Kind of looked like a man. She was carrying a black leather bag."

The boy looked at him, then continued tightening the straps around his package. "Maybe," he said.

Tom dug the quarter out of his pocket and gave it to

the boy, who looked at it disdainfully before jamming it into his jeans.

"Yeah. She went in there." The boy pointed to a low brick building behind a screen of evergreens. The sign on the lawn was too small to read from here.

"Thanks."

The boy hopped on his bike and rode off. Tom walked up the street until he could read the sign:

REED CLINIC
Convalescent Care
Outpatient Therapy

Tom looked at the building. All the windows were covered by blinds. A lawn sprinkler system was soaking the grass in overlapping circles. He smelled wet earth, saw a gardener weeding a flower bed at the far edge of the lawn. It might have been any office building anywhere: modern, unobtrusive, a discreet part of a residential neighborhood. Nothing special at all.

Except that Sylvia was inside.

He started up the wide slate walk. His legs felt unsteady under him. He had to grab twice at the glass door. Inside, the air conditioning left a faint antiseptic smell. He walked over to an alcove and looked in at a woman wearing a nurse's white uniform.

"Yes, can I help you?" Her smile was wide and instant, an automatic welcome.

"I'm here to see Sylvia Macy," he told her. "I'm her brother, Tom Stevens."

There was nothing automatic in her response now. She seemed momentarily confused. "Her brother?"

Tom nodded. Sweat ran down his neck onto his back. "Yes."

169

The nurse put down the papers she had been leafing through. "Will you wait right here?" she asked. She disappeared through a door in the far wall of the alcove. She was gone a long time. When she came back, it was not through the alcove door, but around a corner of the corridor he stood in.

"Please follow me," she said.

She led the way along the corridor, down a few steps to a lower level, past a row of blank doors. The one she stopped in front of was slightly ajar.

"Dr. Spinney will see you in here."

The nurse did not enter in front of him, but held the door open instead. He went inside. Pale light filtered through the blinds across a row of windows high in one wall. A large desk occupied one end of the room. Beside it in a chair, Carlotta Sims sat alone, the black satchel at her feet. She turned as he came in and her face registered her surprise, and then, quickly afterwards, her anger.

"You!" she said.

He stared at her. Behind him, the nurse shut the door.

Chapter Nineteen

"SO YOU DID FOLLOW ME," Carlotta Sims said.

"Yes." Tom was standing under the windows, with half the room between them.

"I thought you might be around somewhere. I was careful."

Tom nodded. "I knew you would be, at first. And I was lucky."

Carlotta grunted. "At least you don't brag about yourself." She moved her chair around so that she did not have to continue craning her neck in order to see him. "Are you really Sylvia's brother Tom?"

"Yes. Why else would I go to all this trouble?"

"Bah!" Carlotta slapped the arm of her chair. "You could be one of Von Webber's spies."

Tom looked at her.

"Oh, you pretend innocence quite convincingly. Where did he hire you? At an acting school?"

Tom shook his head. "I don't know what you're talking about."

"Perhaps not." Carlotta made a noise in her throat as if she were preparing to spit. "Theo Von Webber has been trying to talk your sister into marrying him for years. Ever since she rid herself of that idiot, Willy Macy."

"So why would he hire spies?"

"She tries to hide from him. He uses spies to keep track of her, so that he can lavish expensive gifts on her and wear her down that way. It's a game! But he plays it with deadly seriousness. He is not the sort of man to accept a no answer, even a hundred no answers."

"I'm not one of his spies. Did you keep me from seeing her because you thought I was?"

Carlotta glared at him. "I'd rather you were one of his toads." She stood up and walked to where he was standing. He did not back away, although he wanted to. Her face stopped only inches from his. "Because if you are really Sylvia's brother Tom, then you are the last person I want her to see, the very last."

He stared back at her. "Why?"

"Because it is the past that is eating her up alive and you are part of that past. If you were only safely dead and buried, she would stand a chance of putting it all away for good. But with you here her ghosts will take on the power of flesh and blood."

"I'm not a ghost."

"To Sylvia you are."

"But she's here. And I'll see her now whether you like it or not." As he spoke, the door opened and a stocky, balding man came in. He walked over to where they stood, holding out his hand to Tom.

"I'm Dr. Spinney."

Tom immediately liked the doctor's firm, strong hand-shake. "I'm . . ."

"You're Sylvia's brother Tom," Dr. Spinney interrupted. "The nurse told me. I can't tell you how happy I am to see you."

Tom couldn't resist a quick glance in Carlotta's direction. Her meaty face was cold, expressionless. "When can I see my sister?"

Dr. Spinney sighed. "I wish I knew, Tom. You see, she slipped out of here this morning just before the shift change. She's gone."

Carlotta was incensed. She would not return to her chair beside the doctor's desk. Instead, she paced behind the chair in which Tom was sitting, hurling accusations at Dr. Spinney.

"How could you let her just wander out of here?" she complained. "This is supposed to be one of the best . . ."

"We are not a prison, Ms. Sims," Dr. Spinney said. "We're here to help the people who need us, not lock them up."

"Very noble sentiments, Doctor. Very high-toned. But that does not cover up the fact that Sylvia needed watching and you people blew it."

Dr. Spinney stood up. If he was angry, he was not showing it. "Ms. Sims, I can deal more directly with your understandable disappointment later today. Let's see . . ." He consulted an appointment book on his desk. "I have an open slot at four. Please come back then if you'd like. But now I really must insist on some time alone with Tom.

There are vital questions I need answers to if I'm to help Sylvia at all."

Carlotta returned to her chair long enough to jerk the black satchel out from under it. For a second Tom thought she was going to throw it at the doctor.

"Maybe I should remind you, Dr. Spinney, that I am the one who has been paying Sylvia's bills here."

"That's true."

"Then I am entitled to some respect."

The doctor nodded. "Yes, you are."

"Then start showing it!"

Dr. Spinney scribbled something into his appointment book. "I'll see you at four."

"I will not be here at four."

"Whatever you choose."

"It is not my choice, and you know very well it is not. I have thought all along that you are motivated more by your fat fees than by any of your lovely sounding sentiments."

The doctor nodded. "And I, for one, Ms. Sims, have always wondered if your motives are as pure as you portray them."

"What is that supposed to mean?"

The doctor shrugged. "Just what is the true nature of your relationship with Sylvia?"

Carlotta snorted. At the door she whirled around for one last parting shot. "You, Dr. Spinney, are an incompetent."

When she was gone, Dr. Spinney shook his head. "I'm sorry, Tom. I let that get out of hand. I'm afraid my personal feelings got in the way. She hooks me occasionally with that steamroller approach of hers." The doctor crossed out what he had just written in his appointment book. "I do definitely not like bullies."

Tom smiled. "She's not my favorite person."

Dr. Spinney nodded. "Can you tell me, Tom, what brings you here?"

Tom looked down at his hands. "The whole thing?"

"Yes, as much as you care to share."

"It's a long story."

"I would imagine it is."

"Did . . . did Sylvia tell you things about me?"

The doctor didn't answer him. "Suppose you tell me things about you."

Tom took a long, deep breath. "I used to have these flashbacks," he began, back at the beginning, which seemed like a lifetime ago. "Memories, sort of, only I didn't know they were memories. . . ."

The telling of it began slowly, hesitantly. But as he talked, Tom found that it became easier. The words began to spill out; they went from a trickle to a torrent. Things he had not intended to include came out too, with all the rest, even some things about Alice Blake.

"She's become important to you," Dr. Spinney said.

"Yes, she has." Tom was suddenly stuck, silent. He felt his eyes burning.

"It's okay to care about her, Tom," Dr. Spinney said gently.

"I do, I really do."

"Have you told her?"

"I . . . I . . ." Tom realized he had locked his hands together. He forced them apart. "Not directly."

"You're waiting for her to guess?"

Tom laughed. "No."

Dr. Spinney leaned back in his chair. Sometime during this time he had begun putting down notes on a yellow legal pad. He kept the pen in his hand now as he cradled the back of his head. "Suppose we return to your search for your sister. Have any new memories surfaced since you came to Boston?"

Tom shook his head. "Nothing since I remembered her leaving me at my aunt and uncle's house when I was five. It seems like the doors closed tight after that popped out."

"Nothing at all?"

Tom sat up straight. "Well, I've had dreams."

"Tell me about them."

"There's not much."

Dr. Spinney looked at him, waiting. "Whatever you remember about them."

Tom shrugged. "I dream about a causeway."

"A causeway?"

"Yeah. A long, granite causeway connecting Shepherd Island to the mainland."

"Go on."

"I'm always trying to walk over this causeway to the island, but I never get there. Waves come up and the causeway starts to crumble and I wake up."

Dr. Spinney leaned forward and wrote something on his pad. "And you have this dream, how often?"

"Almost every night."

"Is there such a causeway?"

"Yes." Tom stared at Dr. Spinney. A cold shiver ran up his neck. "I mean, I wondered if it was . . . you know, real. I wasn't sure."

"Until I asked?"

"Yes."

"And Shepherd Island?"

"There is such a place. I've heard it mentioned by people. I looked on a map of Cape Ann. It's there."

"But you don't remember it, except in this dream?"

Tom nodded.

"And in the dream you never get across the causeway? You never reach the island itself?"

"No sir."

"Because you haven't seen Sylvia in eleven, no twelve years? Because you can't find her?"

Tom looked at him. "I don't understand."

Dr. Spinney scratched the back of his hand. "Sylvia's on that island, isn't she, Tom?"

"Yes."

"And the field of your memories, the field by the sea, the field of tall brown grass?"

"That's on the island, too."

"You know all this, Tom, don't you? And yet, you've never thought to go back there and take a look?"

"I was looking for Sylvia here in Boston." Tom felt anger welling up in his throat. "I mean, she's here! I missed her today by a few lousy hours, right?"

"Yes."

"Then why do you make it sound like I've been looking in the wrong place?"

"Do I?"

Tom realized how angry he felt and stopped.

"What are you feeling, Tom?"

Tom started to cry. It went on for a long time, while Dr. Spinney waited, without impatience.

"Let me tell you a little about what I know of your sister," Dr. Spinney said. He again leaned back in his chair. "I've been working with her for some months now, first as an outpatient, the last week or so more intensively while she was staying here."

He paused, looking down across his chest at Tom. "I'm

not going to reveal details. That wouldn't be the way I deal with things my patients tell me in trust. But you *are* her brother and you should know that she has taken it upon herself to accept all the guilt from the family situation. That's not uncommon: the victim blames herself for some-how provoking the acts of others toward her, in this case, your father. She also blames herself for your father's death and she can't forgive herself for leaving you with your aunt and uncle. She has bouts of severe depression that totally incapacitate her, render her unable to cope with any of the day to day stress we all encounter." He paused again. "She also has moments when she's obsessed with the idea of ending her life."

Dr. Spinney reached into the inside of his jacket and took out a folded piece of paper. He handed it across to Tom. "I'm not trying to alarm you," he said. "But I would a damn sight rather she were here where I could keep an eye on her."

Tom opened the folded piece of paper. "This is from my sister?"

"Yes. She left it in her room this morning."

The handwriting was neat, the individual letters evenly spaced, much more than legible, almost drawn on the paper:

> Dear Dr. Spinney:
>
> I know that you will be angry with me, and I feel badly about that. But we aren't getting any-where and all this endless talking, talking, talk-ing, while you listen and scribble your neat notes, is bumming me out.
>
> I've got to face my private horrors directly once and for all—this material from my past, as

178

you so delicately call it. I've got to go face it and put it away and forget it, for good and for all time.

I won't be back. If I plan any kind of retreat now I won't have the courage to go through with this. I'm sorry to be one of your failures. I know you don't have many. You have my permission to expunge me from the records so that your statistics won't be screwed up.

Think kindly of me. I really tried. But your approach is getting us nowhere. Mine will work—it has to. I shall call up the ghosts one by one and kill them off, forever and forever.

love,
Sylvia

Dr. Spinney gave Tom time to read the letter twice, then he took it back and refolded it neatly along the original creases. "I'm afraid things won't work the way she so devoutly hopes they will."

"She's going back to Cape Ann," Tom said. "To Shepherd Island, to wherever our house was."

Dr. Spinney nodded. "That would be my guess."

Tom stood up. The doctor walked with him to the door.

"Tom, I hope you can talk your sister into returning here," he said. "And I want you to promise me something."

"What?"

"That you'll come back to see me, regardless of what your sister decides."

"You think I need a shrink, too?" Tom realized what he had said and shook his head. "I'm sorry."

Dr. Spinney laughed. "Don't be. I've been called worse things, often by our mutual friend, Carlotta Sims."

"But you think I need . . . treatment?"

"Therapy, Tom. For a few weeks, maybe a few months. You're going through a difficult time. There's no disgrace in being in therapy. Some people even view it as a status symbol."

Tom smiled. "Maybe."

"Think about it." He handed Tom a business card. "One or the other of these telephone numbers will usually reach me." He opened the door and followed Tom out into the corridor. "In case you get into a jam with your sister."

"Thank you, Dr. Spinney."

They shook hands. "Realize one important thing, Tom," Dr. Spinney said. "The past doesn't have to be a sentence of doom. Remember that."

Tom looked at him. "I will."

"Good." Dr. Spinney slapped him lightly on the shoulder. "Good luck."

Alice listened quietly while he recited to her the details of his interview with Sylvia's doctor. When he was finished, she poured more wine into their glasses. They were sitting in the pub next to her gallery. This early in the evening, most of the booths and tables were empty. A bored waiter leaned against the bar talking to the bartender.

"So you're going to Cape Ann after her?"

Tom nodded. "I'll hitch back to Delmory tonight and get the rest of my money out of the bank tomorrow."

"Take the Fiat."

He looked at her. "What?"

"Take the Fiat. Time could be important." She smiled when she realized he still didn't believe her. "You're trustworthy, honest, upstanding and honorable, aren't you? Why wouldn't I trust you with my car?" She reached across the table and slipped her hand over his. "But if you put so much as a dent in her little red skin, I'll take it out of your hide."

"I'll be careful."

"I'm counting on it," she said.

Outside, the soft blue light of dusk was hovering over the city. They walked slowly to where her car was parked. She handed him the keys.

"You will be driving me home before you go tearing off, won't you?" she asked.

"Of course."

"Well, I wasn't sure." She bit her lower lip. "I never know how a knight in shining armor is going to behave."

"I'm not a knight."

"Perhaps your sister will think you are."

She switched on the radio as they drove across town. She found a quiet station, hummed along with the song they were playing. When he noticed her gazing his way several times, he remembered Dr. Spinney's comments about her. He wanted to tell her now how he felt, but he couldn't decide on the words.

"Can you drive into the garage and come up for a while?" she suddenly asked. "Or do you have to be off right away?"

He turned onto the street behind her apartment building and stopped. He waited while she fumbled with the remote control device.

"You don't have to come in," she said angrily. "I wouldn't want to delay you."

"Stop it," he said. He took the remote control out of her hands, pushed the button and watched the garage door slowly open. He gunned the engine and drove into the dimly lit parking area. He parked the Fiat in her spot and switched off the engine.

"I love you," he said.

She laughed. "You don't have to announce it as if it were a social disease."

"Is it funny?" he asked.

She shook her head. "No, it's not. I always laugh when . . ." She stopped in midsentence.

"When what?"

"When someone scares me." She reached over and touched his face. "And Tommy, you scare the hell out of me."

Mrs. McDougle stopped him in the hallway outside her door. "I believe your room rent is due today, Mr. Stevens."

"I'm leaving," he told her. "Tonight. I have my deposit coming, right?"

"I have to check your room first," she said quickly. "No telling how much damage you've done."

"Okay. I'll be cleared out of it in ten minutes."

It only took him five minutes to gather up his things. He had two copies of the drawing of Sylvia left. He took one and wrote on the bottom of it:

> Paul,
>   I have to leave town for a while. I'll be back.
> I'll see you again.
>
> Tom

He went out into the hall and slipped the drawing under Paul's door. He hoped Paul could read. If not, he hoped there was someone who would read it to him. He did not want to disappear.

Mrs. McDougle arrived to inspect his room. She made an elaborate procedure of it, stopping before several gouges in the walls.

"That was there when I moved in," Tom told her each time. Finally she took some bills out of her apron pocket and handed them to him folded. She started out the door.

"This is only half what I gave you," he told her.

"That's all I can refund," she said without turning around. "You're supposed to give me a week's notice. Think I can just rent this room out tomorrow?"

She was still grumbling when she reached the stairs. He did not go after her. He guessed she was cheating him out of the money, but he didn't have time tonight for a battle with her. He wanted to reach Delmory before Aunt Belle and Uncle Carl went to sleep.

He jammed the bills she had given him into a pocket of his jeans and picked up his suitcase and laundry bag. Outside, on the street, Alice Blake's red Fiat awaited him.

He hurried downstairs and out the front door. Mrs. McDougle leaned out one of her windows and watched him throw his luggage into the car.

As he climbed into the car, he waved up to her. "I told you I'm rich, Mrs. McDougle," he shouted.

She slammed her window down. He gunned the engine and left Turnbull Street behind.

Chapter Twenty

It was nearly midnight when he drove into the driveway in Delmory. There was a light on upstairs, and Uncle Carl heard the car and came down to see who it was, switched on the porch light and let him in.

"Tom!"

"Sorry it's so late, Uncle Carl. I . . ."

His uncle shook his hand and pulled Tom through the door. "Damn the hour! Who cares? Let's look at you, boy. How are you? You haven't called us in over a week. Your aunt . . ."

"Tom!"

Aunt Belle was flying down the stairs, her robe billowing, her slippers barely touching the steps. He kissed her. They made him come into the kitchen and sit down while Aunt Belle made tea, sliced an entire coffee cake into large pieces and put two of them on a plate in front of him.

"You're a sight for my eyes," she said two or three times. "I'm not ashamed to admit we've been worried about you. Why didn't you call more often? Did Wayne find you?"

Uncle Carl came in with his suitcase and laundry bag. "Well, Tom, who owns the sports car?"

"A friend. She loaned it to me to drive . . ." He realized that Aunt Belle believed he was home for good; perhaps they both did. He stood up, his mouth full of coffee cake and hugged her. "I'm not done yet. Sylvia's on Cape Ann. I'm going there tomorrow. I came back to get the rest of my money, ask you a few questions. And to see you, of course," he added, realizing it was already too late to add anything.

Aunt Belle pulled away from him and returned to the stove, where the water kettle was boiling. "Well, of course, we know you'll keep looking till you find her." She poured water into Tom's cup. "Carl?"

"Nothing for me, Belle." He settled his large frame into a chair and watched Tom fiddle with his tea bag. "So Sylvia is on the Cape?"

Tom nodded. "I'm almost certain of it." He explained as briefly as he could what he had learned from Dr. Spinney and the note Sylvia had left behind at the clinic. They did not look impressed.

"Seems like very little to go on," Aunt Belle said.

"It's a whole lot more than I've had before," Tom told them.

"What if she's not there?" Uncle Carl asked.

"She will be. She has to be. Nothing else makes any sense."

Uncle Carl grunted. "That's what I mean. You're riding for a fall. Your hopes are pretty high. How bad are you going to feel if you're wrong, if she isn't there? Or she's there but you can't find her?"

Tom tried to hide the anger he suddenly felt toward

185

them. He didn't know why they were trying to shoot him down. "That's why I'm here," he said. "I need to know where my old house was."

Aunt Belle looked at Uncle Carl. "It's been so long. I don't know if we could find the spot again if we went looking for it ourselves, much less . . ."

Tom went out to the car, rummaged through the glove compartment, found the map he wanted and brought it back with him into the kitchen. He unfolded it on the table, pushing the plates and cups out of the way. He tapped the enlarged square that showed Cape Ann jutting out into the Atlantic.

"Just show me where it was: Gloucester, Rockport, north side of the Cape, south side? How far back from the shore? Was it near one of these inlets? Was it on a point of land like," he ran his finger over the map, "this one?"

They studied the map. The longer they went over it, the more unsure they became. He watched them with growing frustration.

"There's Shepherd Island," he said, pointing to a small island just off the northwest shore of the Cape. "Was it near there?"

Aunt Belle shook her head. "It wasn't near the water. There was a dirt road." She looked at her husband. "More like a path through the brush, wasn't it, Carl?"

Uncle Carl nodded. "I remember there was an old quarry nearby where you kids used to swim, at least Sylvia did." He put his finger on a blank place in the middle of the Cape. "I think it was up in here somewhere. The back roads aren't on this map."

"Near a quarry?"

"Yes." Uncle Carl rubbed his eyes. "But as I remember, there are lots of old quarry holes in that section of the Cape."

"Great."

"We're trying!" Aunt Belle snapped.

He looked at her and nodded. "I know." He refolded the map and slipped it into his back pocket. He went over to the stove and turned on the gas under the kettle. "More tea, Aunt Belle?"

"Maybe a touch. Use the same bag. I don't want it too strong."

When the water boiled, he refilled her cup, then his own. The clock on the wall above the refrigerator read after one.

"We thought," Aunt Belle began. "At least I did . . ." She looked into her teacup. "We thought you might get discouraged in time, give it up and come home."

"I've got to find her."

She nodded. "We understand."

The next morning as soon as the bank opened, he took all but ten dollars from his savings account. Before he left town, he drove by Wayne's house and found him mowing the front lawn. Wayne shut the motor off as Tom walked toward him over the piles of grass clippings.

"Every time I think I've got this damn lawn cut back and killed for the season," Wayne grumbled, "it rains and brings the grass back to life." He looked at the Fiat parked by the curb. "Where'd you get *that*?"

"A friend is letting me use it for a few days."

"A friend?" Wayne studied him. "Does he have a name, or is that a secret, too?"

Tom flushed as he picked up the hostility coming from Wayne. "Her name is Alice Blake."

"Alice. A girl even. And if she lets you use her car, what else does she let you . . ." Wayne didn't finish. "Sorry, that was a cheap shot."

"I know, it was."

Wayne glared at him. "Well, if you'd start acting like your old self instead of being so goddamn closemouthed about everything."

"I'm not my old self."

Wayne shrugged. "I guess that's true." He kicked the lawn mower. It rolled a few inches away. "Have you decided who you *are* going to be?"

Tom wanted to shake him, tell him to stop being so angry. He wanted to tell Wayne they would always be friends. . . .

"Found your sister yet?"

Tom shook his head. "But I'm close. I'm only a day behind her now."

"That's great." Wayne scooped up a handful of grass and threw it into the air. "And then what happens? Do the two of you ride off into the sunset together, never to be heard from again?"

"I don't know."

Wayne nodded. "Well, old buddy, I got this damn lawn to finish. I don't need my mother on my case today."

"Okay." Tom backed away. "I'll see you."

"Yeah, see you." Wayne bent over and pulled the starter cord. The mower roared into life. With a quick wave, he walked off, guiding the mower ahead of him toward the far side of the lawn, missing his last cut by several feet. Tom watched for a moment, then returned to the car.

He stepped hard on the accelerator on his way out of town. The Fiat raced through the streets, taking him away, taking him away. . . .

On the highway he let the car go, holding the wheel with fingers that had turned white, until the anger had run its course and the hurt had settled into an ache that he could live with. Only then did he ease up on the gas and return to a normal speed, and by then Delmory was miles behind him.

Chapter Twenty-one

HE REACHED CAPE ANN shortly before noon. Getting off the highway with the idea of finding a road that would take him into the interior, he made the wrong choice and soon found himself on a shore road, several large, impressive resort hotels on his left, the ocean booming over the ledges on his right. A sea wind blew over him, smelling of salt and wet rocks, and as he passed a cove, of mud and kelp.

He pulled off the road and studied his map. Last night in Delmory, he had drawn an X in the blank middle of the Cape, to represent his old house. He realized that drawing an arbitrary X was one thing, finding the house would be something else. The roads on the map circled the shore-line, except for one that cut off one corner. Everything within this circle was empty space. . . .

For hours he drove the shore roads, exploring every dirt

side road that promised entry to the interior, walking up the paths he couldn't drive. He emerged unexpectedly into people's backyards, discovered old cottage colonies and new developments, followed roads that looped back on themselves or came to abrupt dead ends. He was chased by dogs, insulted by people jealous of their privacy, frustrated by gates and fences. He stumbled upon two abandoned quarries that promised success at last, only to find in each case that the roads around them led nowhere else, that no burned out ruins lay close by. He talked to people he met, asked questions everywhere, but for nothing: the summer people didn't know what he was talking about and the natives didn't remember.

In desperation, he drove several times through Rockport, even through the crowded, fish-smelling streets of Gloucester. He was trying to pick up signs of a trail twelve years old, searching for a clue to memories still, for the most part, locked away inside his head.

By late afternoon he had a blinding headache from the sun, stomach cramps from hunger. He had not experienced so much as a flicker of recognition of anything he had seen during all of this long, bewildering day.

Driving through the villages on the north shore of the Cape as the sun settled into a bank of brass-colored clouds, he passed a sign nearly illegible under its rust. He had probably driven by it two or three times during the day, but this time something in the letters caught his attention and he stopped, backed up, and took time to spell it out:

Shepherd Cove

A narrow lane led off to the right, toward the sea. He drove between two granite pillars, bumped slowly down the lane through a tangle of low, vine-laden trees. Was he in desperation looking for signs of the familiar where none existed, or did he actually guess a few moments before he drove out of the trees that this side road led to the causeway to Shepherd Island?

Afterwards, he couldn't be sure. He stopped the car and gazed out over the narrow line of granite blocks that stretched to the island lying low and marshy in the distance. Rows of new summer homes almost, but not quite, succeeded in hiding from his view the fields, the brown grass fields, he had seen in his mind all these years.

He climbed out of the car and stood above the causeway, looking out. He knew he was staring at the familiar. His mouth filled with a bitter taste. At the end of the causeway lay Shepherd Island, the Shepherd Island of now and today but also of the past, his past.

The sea wind blew across his face, but his attention was on the distant fields where the same wind drove broad furrows through the grass. The past and the present now touched, in him. There the island waited for him, and there too, perhaps, he would find Sylvia, at last.

To his right, the lane now led across a dirt parking area to a wider asphalt road and a wider causeway that had been constructed on tons and tons of fill. He got behind the wheel of the Fiat and steered through the pot holes to the new road and drove across the new causeway onto the island.

If his memories were accurate and Shepherd Island was raw wilderness twelve years ago, a lot of development had occurred since. The road he found himself on ran the entire length of the island, perhaps a distance of a mile and a half, past a dozen side roads and two or three hundred summer homes. The fields now for the most part were divided into back yards.

Near a beach he was caught in a traffic jam that shunted him onto a side street that led to a restaurant built on a new pier. Giving up on the traffic for now, he parked the Fiat and entered the restaurant. He found an empty table near the back, ordered fried clams, sipped a lukewarm Coke while he waited for his supper.

The restaurant was crowded. All the tables along the wall of windows that faced on the water were occupied, most of them by families with children. A young couple held hands to his left, the red candle on their table the only one burning in the early evening light. Beyond them, closest to the windows, a woman wearing a straw hat sat over a drink, sketching on her napkin.

The couple holding hands made him think of Alice Blake. He tried not to watch them. When the waitress brought his clams, he ordered another Coke.

The loving couple left while he ate. Their place was taken by a solitary man who immediately tried to strike up a conversation with the woman in the straw hat. She rebuffed him with a shake of her head. Tom was too far away to hear what she said. The solitary man did not persist.

As he ate Tom tried to decide what he would do next. It would soon be too dark to go on looking for the place where he had once lived. But if he came back here tomorrow and wandered the fields that were still wild and open, perhaps he would be able to make himself remember. Forcing himself to focus on the five-year-old boy he had once been might start a new crack in the wall between him and his memories.

And through that crack might he not be able to find his way back to the place where he and Sylvia and their father had lived so long ago?

The prospect of doing this frightened him. But what choice did he have? All the clues were in the past, locked away in memories he had suppressed since he was five. He would have to find a way here on Shepherd Island to shake these memories free. . . .

The woman who had been sketching on her napkin was standing up, preparing to leave. As she retied the ribbon from her straw hat under her chin, the solitary man again said something to her.

"No," she said, loudly enough this time for Tom to hear her. She pulled dark sunglasses out of a shoulder bag and put them on, despite the fading of the evening light. She avoided the solitary man by cutting around Tom's table on her way to the front of the restaurant. It was only after she was gone that he wondered why she had looked familiar.

One of the waitresses was already clearing the woman's table. Tom rushed over and snatched the napkin from her tray. He found the woman's sketch on the back: a few skillful lines drawn in pencil. They showed a girl with long hair playing a guitar, around her a suggestion of grass, and in the grass a line or two that might be the face of a small boy. . . .

"Do you mind?" the waitress complained.

Tom looked at her a moment, then dropped the napkin on her tray.

As he ran by his table, Tom threw down a ten dollar bill. Outside, the pier was crowded with people out walking, their attention drawn across the water toward a pale moon rising. He raced by them, searching for the woman in the straw hat. He spotted her at last near the corner of the main road. She was walking slowly away, her shoulder bag canted at an angle under arm.

He wanted to yell, Sylvia, wait up, wait for me. Instead, he followed her, staying behind her as she walked around the corner and started back along the road toward the causeway. She seemed wrapped up in her own thoughts, oblivious of the people she passed coming the other way, toward the pier. Tom gradually closed the distance between them, certain that she did not know he was there; until, in sight of the causeway, where the road was empty

193

except for the two of them, he was surprised when she suddenly turned toward him.

"Why are you following me?"

He stopped a few feet away. He did not consciously choose his answer. "Because you're my sister Sylvia."

He might have remained silent for all the appearance she gave of hearing him. She turned, and leaving the road, she cut across a bulldozed building site, heading for a row of low sand hills. As if in a trance, he stood there and watched her walk away until she was almost out of sight, fading into the gloom of evening shadows under the brow of the sand hills. He did not catch up with her again until he reached the hills himself, and her silhouette against the glow in the western sky betrayed her presence. She was sitting at the top of one small rise, gazing at the water.

"How do you know who I am?" she asked as he came up.

Here, the only sounds were the beating of his heart and the stray sea wind, dying now in the tops of the dry grass.

"I've been looking for you for weeks. In Boston, and here."

"And what if I told you I'm not this Sylvia of yours, this sister you seem to think I am?" Her voice was low, coming from deep in her throat. "What if I told you you're wrong?"

"I wouldn't believe you."

Suddenly she turned toward him and pulled off her hat. "Then come closer," she said. "Look at my face and tell me that you're sure."

He joined her at the top of the hill. Crouching beside her, he gazed at the shadows of her face. She had removed her sunglasses now, but he could not see her eyes, only the curve of her mouth, a thatch of her short hair, a small crescent along the line of her chin. He stared at her for a long time.

"If you're not Sylvia, who are you?" he asked.

"A figment of your imagination," she said. "I'm not really here at all."

"I saw the drawing you made on your napkin back at the restaurant. It's the same as your paintings."

She sighed. It was a weary sound; she might have been an old woman, for all he could see of her in the dark.

"And so you've caught me," she said.

"Caught you?"

She reached out and took both his hands. Her fingers were like ice on his skin. "Oh yes, Tom. Caught me good and proper." She turned her head toward the sea. "And here of all places."

He peered through the darkness, trying to read her face.

"All these years," she said in her tired, old woman's voice, "I thought of you each and every day, and the one thing I've most dreaded, of all things I've dreaded, is that you might remember, and someday come looking for me."

He pulled his hands away. His disappointment was suddenly too large to be ignored, and with it came a rage that made him want to reach through the shadows and choke her.

"Why didn't you go to Australia then?" he demanded. "If you really hated the idea of ever seeing me again, why did you stay in Boston?"

The dry sound she made then might have been a laugh. "Dr. Spinney would say that I really wanted you to find me after all."

In the silence that fell between them now, Tom could hear, far off over the water, a buoy ringing with the waves. The air had gone cold and damp.

Sylvia took his hands again. "Because in all this time," she said, "I've never stopped loving you, and never stopped hating me."

As they walked back along the island road to where he had

left the car, she asked him no questions about himself, nor did she ask how he had found her. It was as if she didn't want to know, as if she avoided details because she thought they were like little wire traps that might catch her fast to him. Carefully, she kept a few feet between them and avoided his eyes until, on the pier, now almost deserted, she stopped near the Fiat and faced him with a smile that he saw clearly in the light from the front door of the restaurant.

"You could drive off and leave me here," she said. "Wouldn't that be better?"

Again he felt wild rage filling his throat. "I want to ask you some questions," he said coldly.

"I imagine you do," she said. "That, as dear Dr. Spinney would say, is the crux of the issue. I'd like not to answer them."

"I can't force you," he said.

"But you are." She walked around the car to the passenger side and got in. "I'm staying at a motel back toward the highway. It's a dump, but everything else was full."

He started the engine. "You don't have a car?"

"No. I took the train."

As he drove toward the causeway, he told her how he had spent the whole day trying to find the place where they had lived.

"The house burned down," she said.

"I know."

"I'll take you out there tomorrow," she said. "If you're sure that's what you want."

"I'm sure," he told her. "I can't very well turn back now, can I?"

She didn't answer. She sat in the seat beside his and watched the road, her straw hat clutched in her lap, her fingers slowly turning it, bending the brim back on itself until the straw fibers began to break, one by one.

Chapter Twenty-two

SYLVIA'S MOTEL was outlined by garish orange lights. The row of cabins was set close to the road, and the Fiat's headlights were caught in the cabin windows and reflected back as they drove up.

"There it is," Sylvia told him. "My cabin is number eight."

In front of the office, two spotlights illuminated a large sign:

TESSIE'S MOTEL
RESTAURANT
Cabins by day,
week, season.
VACANCY

Several of the words flickered on the edge of extinction.

Tom parked in front of Sylvia's cabin and then walked back to the office. The plump woman watching television there told him she had one empty cabin.

"But the water's shut off in the toilet," she said. "Had a leak and I can't get it fixed till Friday."

"No problem," he said. "I can use the bathroom in my sister's cabin."

"You sure?"

Tom nodded.

Tessie climbed up out of her chair and waddled over to the desk. "I'll knock five dollars off. Only reason I'm even renting it to you is on account there probably ain't another empty room on the Cape tonight." She pushed a card across the desk for him to fill out.

"Your sister, you said?"

"Yes." He leaned toward the door and looked down the row of cabins. "She's in cabin eight."

"Why don't you just stay in her room?"

Tom shrugged and went on filling in the card.

Tessie stared at him as she handed him his change. "Oh, I get it. She really is your sister."

Tom nodded and hurried out. Halfway to his cabin, he heard the screen door to the office creak open.

"Mr. Stevens!"

He looked back.

"If you want to stay after tonight, I've got to know by tomorrow noon."

"Okay."

"Need anything, give a yell." The screen door creaked shut again.

He took his suitcase into his cabin, gave everything a quick inspection, then walked back to cabin eight. Sylvia was just coming out of the bathroom, drying her face in a towel.

"Did she have a vacancy?"

Tom nodded. "But the bathroom is out. I'll have to use yours."

"Sure." Sylvia rubbed her face hard in the towel, then draped it over the back of a chair. "I paid her through the end of the week." She waved a hand at the dingy furniture, the faded paneling curling away from the walls. "Can you believe that? Almost every cent I had on me, but she made it sound as if there wouldn't be another open room on the Cape until fall." She walked to the front door and looked out as a car drove in and parked two cabins down.

"Yeah, I know," Tom said. "She told me I just rented the last one."

Sylvia laughed. "The successful sales through utter panic technique." She turned from the door, looked at Tom, then looked away. "And panic was certainly the state I was in yesterday, wondering why I was here, what I had come for, and the damned taxi sitting out there in the yard running up my bill. . . ."

She opened her shoulder bag, took out a package of cigarettes, waved them toward Tom before taking one herself and lighting it. Tom noticed that her hands were trembling.

"Why did you come here?" he asked.

"I told you, it was the only place that wasn't full." She stared at him when she realized this wasn't what he was asking. She breathed out a cloud of smoke. "Why do you keep looking at me that way?"

He looked away, switched on the television set, switched it off. "I was wondering why I didn't recognize you at that restaurant."

"And?"

He shrugged. He had never imagined while turning Boston upside down looking for her, that once he found her it would be so hard to talk to her. Everything she said seemed faintly hostile, even her laugh just now by the doorway. . . .

"I don't look the way you remember me?"

"I expected that. It's been years since . . ." He slumped into a wooden chair, stared down into his hands. "I knew what you looked like from a drawing I was given, and that drawing does look like you, but . . ." He glanced up at her face, wreathed by smoke from her cigarette. "But you don't look like the drawing."

In the silence he wondered what she was thinking, wondered if she had any idea how uncomfortable she made him. "Do you know what I mean?" he asked at last.

"I don't meet your expectations." Her voice was flat, colorless, not curious at all.

"No, I don't mean that," he said. He was drowning in his own confusion, wishing more than anything else just now that he could find a way out of this conversation and out the door, back to his own cabin. "The drawing looks like you, but it leaves out so much that I see now, in your face." He stood up so quickly that the chair fell over. "That's why I didn't recognize you in the restaurant. If you hadn't been sketching on your napkin, if I hadn't seen the sketch . . ."

Sylvia put out her cigarette in an ashtray on the bureau. "How observant of you, how unfortunate for stupid me."

He covered his feelings by bending down to retrieve the chair. He backed quickly toward the door, but the words came out anyway: "You're really pissed off, aren't you?"

She shook her head. "No, not pissed off."

"You wish to hell our paths hadn't crossed, there in the restaurant."

"Something like that." She fumbled for another cigarette with hands that shook so badly she dropped the pack and had to pick up the cigarettes that rolled onto the floor.

He didn't help her. Instead, he used this moment of distraction to slip out the door.

The orange lights still burned beside each cabin, giving the yard the appearance of a delinquent carnival. In the cross shadows he stumbled over a small dog, sending it yelping back across the yard to where its owner stood stargazing outside the cabin next to his.

"Watch it there!" the man called.

Tom hurried by him into the darkness of his own cabin. But the orange light followed him even into the shadows there, like a flow of thin, sick blood that wouldn't leave him, a pursuing stain that wouldn't go away.

During the night he dreamed that the motel caught fire, that Sylvia came to the door of his cabin to wake him, to warn him of the flames, but stood instead watching him as the fire roared through the walls, onto the bed sheets, over him in a fury while she stared at him from the doorway, silent, watching. . . .

He woke up choking. He was covered with sweat. He stood up and walked to the door, opened it and looked out. The lights still burned outside, but the road beyond was empty.

Back in bed, he tried to forget the dream, but it wouldn't leave him. Early in the morning, when the sky was still gray, the sun still below the horizon, he pulled on his jeans and walked to Sylvia's cabin to use her bathroom. He found her door unlocked, her room empty. He thought at first she had slipped away during the night, but then he realized her things were still in the room, her shoulder bag on the back of one chair, an open suitcase on top of another.

He turned to face the yard and saw movement inside the motel office. He hurried over and found the plump woman pouring herself a cup of coffee. She looked surprised to see him at the door and motioned for him to come inside.

"You must be a lousy sleeper like me," she said. She nodded toward the coffee pot. "Want a cup?"

He shook his head. "Have you seen my sister?"

She stared at him blankly.

"Short hair, pale complexion, pretty. Sylvia Macy, in cabin eight."

"Oh yes, the lady who arrived in a taxi."

"Have you seen her this morning?"

Tessie nodded. "She went for a walk, I guess, down toward the water. About twenty minutes ago, when I first got up."

Tom looked out toward the road. "Which way is the water?"

"Go up the curve in the road about a hundred yards. There's a paved lane that cuts down the embankment to an old coast guard station. It's been abandoned for years. You can reach a small beach there, and then get out on the rocks. If that's where she went. Most everybody likes to get right out to the water and . . ."

"Thanks," Tom said and returned to his cabin for his sneakers. Then, following Tessie's directions, he walked out to the road and turned right. When he reached the paved lane, he could see the coast guard station at the bottom of the embankment. Beyond it, the water of the inlet was still gray, but further out, the ocean glowed with rose reflections from the sunrise.

For a moment he almost turned back, afraid Sylvia would resent his following her on her walk. He could talk to her later when she returned to her cabin.

But he continued on. As he trotted down the lane toward the coast guard station, he reached a point that gave him a clear view into the observation tower at the top of the building. There were two open windows in each side of the tower and Sylvia was sitting in one of these windows facing the water, her back toward him.

He froze, his feet sliding to a stop on the loose pebbles on the pavement. As he watched, Sylvia shifted her weight and dropped one hand out of sight. She looked as if any moment she might let go with her other hand and slip out the window, to fall to the beach below.

He started to yell to her, then realized that yelling would give her too much time, too much warning that he was there. Instead, he ran the rest of the way down the embankment and across a sandy courtyard. He found the door standing open, half buried in sand. He climbed inside, into the darkness there, and stumbled onto the stairs.

He passed two landings on his way up. The observation tower was above the fourth floor, reached by a ladder that rose from the final landing. He climbed the ladder slowly, not wanting to frighten Sylvia, but frightened himself that she might have already fallen to her death. Running so furiously up the stairs, would he have even heard her fall?

He pulled himself in a crouch up onto the floor of the observation room. Sylvia was still there, outlined in the rectangle of one open window, silhouetted against the glowing morning sky. She was holding the window frame with one hand, sitting precariously on the very edge of the sill.

"Sylvia," he whispered. "Please."

Her body stiffened. She turned toward him slightly. "Tom," she said.

He stood up and walked slowly toward her. The room

was full of wind because of the open windows on every side. She shifted her weight, swung her legs in, dropped to the floor beside him.

"You're up early," she said.

He stared at her, wondering what was true, what was false, not sure now how much his fear that she was about to jump from the window had been her intentions, how much his imagination.

"Did you think I was going to jump?" she asked.

"Yes, I did," he said finally.

She shivered and looked out the window, at the beach below, at the water licking its edge. "I would never hurt myself that much," she said. "I hate physical pain."

They exchanged a long look, her eyes intently staring into his.

"Come on," she said. "I'll take you out to the old homestead. You said you wanted to go there."

She brushed by him on her way to the ladder. He did not abandon the tower until she was safely down on the landing below.

Chapter Twenty-three

THEY ATE BREAKFAST in a roadside diner near the motel. Tom stole several looks at Sylvia as they ate, and out in the open car as they drove away from the diner, he suddenly thought how pretty she was despite the pallor of her face.

The paleness, in fact, gave her the fragile look of a china doll, in the same way that her large eyes and full mouth made her seem very approachable. The man last night at the restaurant had obviously thought so, the man who had tried twice to engage her in conversation.

What had Alice Blake told him about Sylvia? *Men want to rush out and do battle with her dragons.*

Tom thought he understood this remark now.

The top was down; the sun poured into the car. "You still have gold highlights in your hair," Tom said. "Even though it's so much shorter and darker now."

Sylvia took out a cigarette, pushed the lighter on the dash. "I've worn it short since . . . for a long time now." She glanced at him as she held the lighter to her cigarette with trembling hands. "How much to you remember?"

He shrugged. "Not much. I remember your long, golden hair, the lullaby you used to sing to me, the fields on Shepherd Island, the night you left me in Delmory."

She looked at her cigarette. "You were crazy about my hair. I used to tell you there was a secret place where I washed it in a stream of liquid gold. And you'd nag me and nag me to take you there so that you could see it for yourself, but of course, I never could."

"I believed you?"

"Yes, you were always so gullible. I could tell you anything, you'd always believe me."

"I loved you madly."

Sylvia nodded. "I could tell you anything."

"Do you still play the guitar?"

Sylvia pushed her cigarette into the ashtray. "No, I don't. Haven't for years."

"Do you remember the lullaby you sang to me?"

There was a long pause before she answered. "Yes." She ran her fingers over the dashboard. "Nice car. Is it yours?"

Tom knew she was trying to change the subject. "No, a friend of mine let me borrow it."

Sylvia nodded. "Take a right here."

As Tom turned the car off the main road, she took out another cigarette.

"Do you remember this road?" she asked.

Tom looked at the trees closing in around them. "No."

"And our father? Do you remember anything about him?"

Tom shook his head. "No, I don't."

206

The road became narrower, the ruts deeper. Tom had to drive slowly to avoid scraping the bottom of the car. As they climbed farther and farther from the main road, the trees thinned until finally they reached high fields of grass interspersed with outcroppings of ledge. The sun flashed on specks of mica in the rock; birds flew from the bushes as they passed. There was the smell of warm vegetation, a sense of emptiness.

"I missed this road yesterday," Tom told her. "I thought I tried them all."

The road petered out completely below a sandy rise. Tom parked the car in the shade provided by a clump of high, leafy bushes.

"Where's the quarry?" he asked.

Sylvia glanced at him, then pointed off to the right. "Over there. Do you remember it?"

"No. Uncle Carl told me there was one close to our house."

They left the car and Sylvia led the way to a gully that rain had cut into the rise. As they climbed, Tom paused several times, looking for something familiar in all of this wild landscape, searching for a view, a tree, a shadow that might strike a chord in his memory.

"Come on," Sylvia called to him. "We're nearly there."

He hurried to catch up with her. "I was seeing if I could remember any of this."

"It's grown over a lot," she told him. She stopped and looked down at him from her stance higher in the gully. Her face glistened with sweat. "Don't force it. You'll remember what you want to remember."

At the top of the rise, Tom saw a blue rim of ocean in the distance.

"You can see the water from here."

Sylvia nodded. "Barely." She did not stop then, but continued on across a granite shelf toward a circle of low, wind-ravaged trees. Sweaty and hot from the hard climb, he shivered now in the cool wind that blew over the top. Beyond the first trees she stopped, and when he reached her, he saw a chimney rising from a thicket of bushes and beyond it, a flight of stone steps, leading up to nothing.

"This is it," Sylvia said. She coughed and leaned against a tree to catch her breath. "I have to sit down."

They found a place to sit on a rock close to the steps. Moss grew in the cracks between the granite blocks that made up the stairway. Now Tom could see, nearly covered by the growth of weeds, other granite blocks that must have once formed the foundation of the house.

"This was the front yard," Sylvia said. Her hands stretched out in front of her, indicating the boundaries of the yard, now reclaimed by wild things.

"And the rabbit pens?"

She looked at him.

"I saw some in one of your paintings."

"Over there. We had three of them. Your favorite you named Tad, from a book I read to you." She studied him. "Do you remember how you cried when father . . . when your rabbit died?"

He shook his head, but a strange, wary feeling was growing in the pit of his stomach. He stood up and walked to the stairway. "Did you read to me a lot?" he asked.

"Yes. You couldn't get enough and when we ran out of books, I made up stories."

" 'The Lost Princess'?"

"Yes, and . . ."

" 'The Frog Kid,' I remember." He ducked into the bushes and lost his breakfast. When he came out by the stairs again, she was still sitting on the rock.

"Are you all right?" she asked.

He nodded. "The story about the Frog Kid, that was about me, right?"

"Yes, you made me put you in a story."

He looked around at the decaying trees. The wind rattled their branches. "I made you put me in a story. I remember how angry I was when it didn't work."

"When what didn't work?"

"I didn't disappear, into the story."

"Oh, so that was why you used to get so upset over that one. I never could get you to explain what was wrong."

"Yeah." Tom took a deep breath, tried to force the weight from his chest. "I thought there was a kind of magic story that if it was about you, you could get right inside it."

Tears were running down Sylvia's face. "Let's leave, okay?" she asked. "Haven't you seen enough?"

He shook his head. "No."

While she remained sitting on the rock, as if frozen there by fear, as if taking refuge there against a rising tide, he explored the ruined foundation. His fingers seemed to know the way through a crack between two granite blocks. They came out with several lumps of twisted metal. He walked back and showed them to Sylvia.

"They were toy soldiers," he said. "The fire must have melted them."

She nodded slowly. "Let's go, Tom."

"Not yet. I want to . . ."

"What's the sense of it?" she interrupted. "Why force yourself to remember things you're better off not knowing?"

He looked at her.

"You see, I remember everything, and I wish I didn't."

"Tell me about the fire."

She shook her head. "No."

"Why not?"

"It . . . it was ugly. I hate ugly things."

"How did it start?"

"No, Tom!"

"I want to know."

She rubbed at her eyes. "Father had been drinking. I guess he dropped a cigarette into a box of rubbish. The smoke woke me up. By the time I got to the kitchen, it was . . ."

"No!"

"Yes, Tom. I barely had time to wake you up, get you out of there before the whole house was . . ."

"You're lying!"

"Tom . . ."

He stared at her as if he could see right through her head into the past. His mouth began to water uncontrollably. He had to spit it away. She started to get up from the rock. He pushed her back down.

"Let me go."

He shook his head. "You started the fire."

She looked at him, her eyes wide and staring. "No, I didn't, Tom. Not that."

"But you were in the kitchen. I saw you standing there. I saw the fire getting bigger and bigger and he was lying over the table and you just stood there letting the fire grow and grow and I said, 'Silly, put it out, put it out,' and you turned toward me and saw me in the doorway and all you said was, 'Tom, you're supposed to be in bed'. . . ."

"Stop it!"

"Tell me the truth!" he shouted. "Sylvia, tell me."

She rubbed her face. When she looked at him again, her eyes were swollen, red. "The fire started accidentally. He fell over the table and knocked the ashtray into the garbage."

"But you . . ."

"Let me finish!" She took hold of his shoulders and shook him. "Listen to me. I did not start that fire. He did."

"But you just stood there and watched it!"

She nodded. "I couldn't put it out. I couldn't move. It was like I was nailed to the spot. And all I could think was how much I wanted to be free, free of him . . ."

Suddenly she pulled him close and hugged him. "And then there you were, screaming at me from the doorway, standing there in your torn underwear with that dumb looking teddy bear of yours you were holding onto by one ear. It was too late to put out the fire by then and he . . . and he was still passed out, too drunk to know what was happening. But there was still time to get you out of there alive. I grabbed you and we ran, out the front door, across the yard. By the time we reached the trees, the whole sky was turning red. We stopped to look back; we saw the flames break through the roof."

They held onto each other as she told him about the fire, but he hardly heard her words. Staring over her shoulder he saw, not the overgrown field that had once been their front yard, but the burning house as it had looked that night twelve years ago. He saw the dry roof explode into flames, felt Sylvia's hot, dry hand holding his, pulling him at last away, away into the darkness beyond the fire. . . .

He pulled himself out of her arms. "Why did we leave him there to die?"

Her body stiffened. She pulled up a corner of her shirt and wiped at her eyes.

"Why, Sylvia?"

"You want the truth, I'll tell you," she said in a wooden voice. "Our father was a madman. One day he'd be kind and sweet, crying over the things he'd done to us, the next day he'd get moody, touchy, snap at us for nothing. Then, soon, there would be another drinking binge and the rage would come over him again and he'd do . . . all those terrible things again."

"What things, Sylvia?" Tom whispered.

"Oh, he'd beat you, Tom. For nothing. He'd beat you so bad and I couldn't stop him." Her shoulders shook as she cried. "And when at last you'd cry yourself to sleep, he would come after me . . ." She pushed him back. "I don't want to remember!" she screamed. "I don't!"

He stared at her. Slowly her eyes came up to meet his.

"He used me, Tom. He would forget I was his daughter and he'd . . . he'd use me like a woman. And I was only a skinny, scrawny kid." She pulled open her shirt and pointed to a series of white scars that ran down from her shoulders. "I've got marks of his all over my body."

He turned away, afraid he would be sick again. Behind him, she caught her breath in a series of hiccups.

"You wanted the truth," she said. "That's the truth about our father."

He turned back to face her. She was buttoning her shirt. "I'm sorry," he whispered.

She shrugged. "Why? It wasn't your fault."

"Why didn't you run away sooner?"

"I couldn't leave you behind." She reached out and stroked his face. "Oh, we were a pair back then, you and me, spinning our songs and stories to each other as if our whole world was one happy dream. I'd make a nest for you in the tall grass and hide you there and tell you that you were invisible and you'd believe me, every time. Oh, I could tell you anything."

She pulled her hand away.

"Let's go back to the car," she said.

212

As they headed toward the gully that would take them down to where they had parked the car, Tom looked back at the bare chimney, rising like a broken monument to all that had been here and now was gone. The chilly sea wind blew over his sweaty face and on into the overgrown clearing where once their house had stood. Overhead the tree branches rattled and rubbed against each other with a dry and barren sound.

Sylvia did not wait for him at the top of the rise, but plunged down ahead of him. As he hurried to catch up to her, he had to fight an impulse to run; and as they drove out along the rutted road, his foot continually, as if it had a mind of its own, pressed down too hard on the gas.

"So my name for you was Silly," he said as they drove through heavy traffic back to the motel.

She nodded. "By the time you were old enough to pronounce my name correctly, the nickname had stuck."

He stopped at an intersection, then turned right. "Why did we spend so much time out on Shepherd Island?"

"He painted there a lot. It wasn't developed then."

"Was he any good?"

"As a painter?"

"Yeah."

She shrugged. "He was popular for a while. A few museums and collectors bought his work, before the accident that killed Mom. After that..." She glanced at him, reached for a cigarette. "I've never gone to see any of his paintings."

At the motel he parked in front of her cabin.

"Do you have any change?" she asked.

He reached into his pocket and brought out a handful. She thanked him and walked over to the telephone booth outside the motel office. When he came out of her cabin after using the bathroom, she was just finishing her call. She walked slowly across the yard toward him.

"I just called a friend of mine," she said. "He's coming to get me this evening."

"Who?"

"His name is Theo."

The name sounded familiar, but Tom couldn't remember where he had heard it before.

"Theo Von Webber," Sylvia said. "I'm going to marry him."

Then he remembered: Carlotta Sims had accused him of being a spy for Von Webber in Dr. Spinney's office on Tuesday.

"You're going to marry him?" Tom asked.

Sylvia nodded.

"But why?"

"Because he's promised to take me to Europe."

Tom looked at her in total confusion. "I don't understand. We just . . ."

She shook her head. "I came here to see if once and for all I could face my ghosts and put them forever behind me."

He nodded. "I knew that, I . . ."

"I failed. It doesn't work. They don't go away. They don't stop hurting."

"But Dr. Spinney . . ."

"To hell with Dr. Spinney!"

He followed her into her cabin. "What about us?"

"Us?" She looked at herself in the mirror above the bureau, touched her hair. "We're in the past, too."

"No, we're not. We're here, right now."

She shook her head. "Theo will take me away from here. I'll never have to see all this again." She waved a hand around the cabin, but Tom knew she was referring to the clearing and the ruin of the house, to Shepherd Island and the fields of grass.

"It doesn't work that way," he said.

"Now you sound like Dr. Spinney." Her face was chalk white. A line of sweat had formed along her upper lip.

"Please don't go," he said.

"I have to take a nap now," she said. "Theo will be here in a few hours." She lay down on the bed, on her side, facing away from him, one hand pressed tightly between her knees. "I have to sleep now, Tom. Please wake me when Theo comes."

He stood there awhile, but she said nothing more. Her white face was pressed against the pale pillowcase, her wide and lovely eyes were closed. He could not bring himself to wake her, to argue with her further, and so he went outside and found a chair to sit in beside her door, and settled down in it to wait for Theo.

Chapter Twenty-four

AT NOON he remembered that he had paid for only one night in his cabin. He went to the motel office and paid for another night. Back at Sylvia's door, he resumed his perch in the chair.

Throughout the afternoon other guests came and went in their cars, stirring up clouds of dust that drifted across the yard to settle on the trees overhanging the cabins. Occasionally Tom looked in on Sylvia to see if she was still sleeping. Each time that he did, he found her on her side as before, her breathing shallow and regular.

Sitting there alone through the long hours, he began to feel as if he were waiting for the world to change sides, for everyone in one place to shift to some place else, while he sat there unmoving, unable to change, unwilling to change.

Sylvia slept as peacefully as a child, waiting for her Theo to come and take her away to Europe, and Theo himself, still a dark and faceless stranger, was coming here, changing the course of his life, changing sides.

Tom used the time to select his arguments. The sea breeze rustled through the leaves above him while cars swept by the motel in an endless stream. He remained in his chair, not willing to give up, not changing.

He heard Sylvia get up and go into the bathroom. By then, the sun was low enough in the sky to cast long shadows across the motel yard. When Sylvia came out of the bathroom, she was singing under her breath, and when he entered the cabin, she smiled at him.

"I was thinking about that lullaby I used to sing to you," she said. "I woke up humming it." She began packing her clothes into the suitcase on the chair. "Did you get in a good nap?"

"No, I didn't," he said.

"Oh, too bad. I feel so much better now. You really should have . . ."

"Sylvia."

She continued folding clothes and pushing them into the suitcase. "What is it, Tom?"

"You're making a mistake. Marry this Theo guy if you want to but go back to the clinic. Go back to seeing Dr. Spinney."

"Why should I do that? Why marry Theo at all if we don't go to Europe?"

"I don't understand."

"I'm not in love with him, Tom. He's been pestering me for years." She turned to face him, leaning back against the bureau.

"But you're going to marry him."

"Yes."

"I don't understand you."

"I'm getting tired of hearing you say that." She returned to her packing, but he reached out and caught her arm.

"If we never see each other again," he told her, "at least give me five minutes now."

She slumped against the bureau. "Very well. You want me to spell it out for you. Fine." She looked around for her cigarettes. "Get me one, will you?"

The pack was on the bed table. He handed them to her. She fumbled for her lighter in her shoulder bag. He waited while she took several deep drags, blowing smoke up toward the ceiling of the cabin. Through the open doorway, Tom saw a gray Mercedes signaling to turn into the motel.

"Tell me why, Sylvia," he said. "Tell me why you'll marry him even though you don't love him."

"Because he'll take care of me. Not just Europe, everything else, too. He'll take care of me. That's all I really ask of anyone now. Is that so terrible?"

He nodded. "I think so."

"And you're an arrogant shit." She ground her cigarette into the ashtray. "Now if you're done playing twenty questions, I have packing to finish. Theo will be here soon."

The gray Mercedes had stopped in front of the motel office. Tom watched a tall man in a light tan suit get out and go to the office door.

"How will Theo be different from William Macy? I'm sure he was perfectly willing to take care of you too, and you couldn't stand him for long."

She looked at him, her eyes cold, furious. "You really have been poking into my life."

"I was trying to find you. I talked to a lot of people."

"I bet you did. Well, for your information, Theo is not another Willy."

"Isn't he?"

Her right hand flew across his face. The slap caught him by surprise, ringing his ears. Her expression suddenly fell apart; the angry, haughty look melted into tears. "Oh Tom, I'm so sorry." She cupped his face in her hands, kissed him. "I'm sorry."

He grabbed her fluttering hands, squeezed them tight. "Change your mind, while there's time. Give us time to know each other again."

"No. I can't. I . . . I don't want to change my mind."

"What about Carlotta?"

Sylvia's face grew hard again. "That possessive bitch! She gave me no peace at all."

There was a firm rap on the screen door. Looking over, Tom saw the tall man in the tan suit.

"Theo!" Sylvia rushed across to let him in. While they kissed, Tom looked away, embarrassed by Sylvia's false show of affection. Then she was pulling on his arm. "Theo, this is my brother Tom. We just . . . we just ran into each other here on the Cape." Sylvia's voice was urgent, breathless, as if she weren't getting enough air. "Tom, this is Theo Von Webber."

As they shook hands, Tom realized that Theo didn't believe her, didn't think for one moment that Tom was her brother. The coldness in his eyes as he looked at them said this. But worse, Tom realized that Theo didn't really care, as long as Sylvia left with him now.

"A pleasure, Tom," Theo said. He was not the old man that Tom had thought he would be, but his face was lined, his hair thinning badly. He was not handsome, not distinguished looking, not even faintly attractive. But there was no denying the expensive cut of his suit, nor the Mercedes parked outside.

He turned now toward Sylvia with a little bow of his head. "Are you ready, love? Is this your suitcase?"

She nodded, her hands trembling so badly she could not shut the latches on the suitcase.

"Let me," Theo told her. He snapped them shut, lifted the suitcase off the chair. "Shall we?"

Sylvia nodded. She picked up her shoulder bag. "I'll be out in a second, Theo. Let me just say good-by to Tom."

Again the little bow as Theo stepped to the door. "I'll wait for you in the car. Don't be long."

"I won't." When he was gone, she grabbed Tom's hands and held them against her chest. "Don't hate me, Tom. Please?"

He hadn't the heart then to fight her any longer. He forced himself to smile. "I don't hate you."

"Sure?"

He nodded. "Yes, I'm sure."

"Poor Tom! You thought all you had to do was find me and then everything would be all right."

"It doesn't matter now."

"Life isn't that simple, is it?"

"No, it isn't."

She kissed his hands. "Good-by, Tom."

He knew he would never see her again and so there was just this one last chance to give her something important and all he could give her was the sight of him standing there letting her go, lightly, without pain.

"Good-by, Sylvia. Enjoy Europe, enjoy it all, all you can get."

She lingered in the doorway. "You'll be okay?"

He nodded. "I'll be fine." He wanted her to hurry,

before his stiff face began to crack. "Go on. Theo is waiting for you."

"I love you, Tom," she whispered and then she dashed for the Mercedes.

Tom forced himself to stand by the door and wave to her, smiling, until Theo had backed the Mercedes around, until he had driven with her onto the road and they were gone. Only then did Tom allow his smile to fade. Standing in the suddenly empty cabin, in the utter silence, he looked around for something to smash, something to break into a thousand pieces, but all he saw was his own reflection in the mirror above the bureau.

"Sylvia," he said out loud. The sound of her name seemed to ring in the room with echoes that went on and on, fainter, softer, emptier, but still on, echoing in the room and in his head and in his heart. . . .

He called Alice Blake from a telephone booth on the highway. When she answered, he said, "I'm on my way back to Boston."

"Tom? Are you all right?"

"Yes."

"Did you find your sister?"

"Yes."

"Well. . ." Alice's voice faltered, faded. "Well, what happened?"

"Tell you when I get there. Sorry it's so late."

"Don't worry about it." Another pause. "And don't break any speed records getting here. I want you in one piece."

"Okay."

"Really, Tommy, just get here when you get here. I'll be awake. Okay?"

"Yes."

He had the gas tank filled, drank a cup of coffee at the counter in the restaurant. Then he drove on toward Boston, through a nighttime filled with music from the car radio, through clouds of white moths that swept over his windshield in helpless ecstasy.

Remembering his promise to Alice, he did not drive fast and he arrived in the city after midnight, in light traffic that made it easy for him to find his way onto the proper exit ramp. On the street behind her apartment building he took the remote control out of the glove compartment and signaled the garage door to open for him.

In the elevator, on his way up to her apartment, he discovered how eager he was to see her. It was as if he had suddenly come back to life, come back from the dead.

"What will you do now?" Alice asked him when he had told her everything that had happened on the Cape. They were sitting on her balcony. She was in her long blue robe; he was still in the sweaty jeans and T-shirt he had worn all day.

"I'm not going to crawl into a hole because of this," he said.

"I didn't think you would."

He looked at her in the dim light from the candles on the glass coffee table, in the glow from the city beyond the balcony. "Dr. Spinney told me the past doesn't have to be a death sentence."

"No, Tommy, it doesn't."

"It will be for Sylvia." A sob tore at his chest. "It will be for Sylvia."

"Maybe not," Alice whispered.

"She should have come back with me and gone on seeing Dr. Spinney. We could . . ." He was choking on his words. "We could have worked it all out."

"Yes, she should have." Alice got up from the hammock

and came over to his chair. "Why the hell don't you go ahead and cry?" she asked.

"I don't want to."

"Bullshit." She rubbed his shoulders. "Denying feelings, that's Sylvia's way, not yours."

He squeezed his hands together until his fingers turned white.

"Are you ashamed of what you feel?"

"No."

"Then don't crawl into that hole. Don't lock your feelings up inside. Goddamn it, Tommy, you know that doesn't work!"

He looked at her through a blur of tears.

"Tommy, dear Tommy, Dr. Spinney is right, your past isn't the end of you, not if you can let go of it." She kissed his face, his eyes, his chin. "Let go of it, Tommy. Let go!"

And he let go, stepped off into space, on faith alone, in the belief that there had to be a far shore out there somewhere, in the belief that he would find it.

She poured them both a glass of wine, then disappeared into the kitchen to reappear a few minutes later with a plate of sandwiches.

"Will you be going back to Delmory?" she asked.

He nodded. "I think I forgot for a while how much Aunt Belle and Uncle Carl care about me, how much I love them. They let me go to find Sylvia even though they didn't think I should do it. They let go of me even though they were afraid I'd never come back. And I want to go back. I want to let them know what they mean to me."

He reached for a sandwich, ate half of it in two bites. "I have another year of high school. And Wayne, my best friend, he's back there too."

"And after high school?" she asked.

223

"College, I guess. I don't know what I want to do for a career." He waved the last of his sandwich toward the balcony wall. "But I know I want to go to school here in Boston."

She smiled. "The city's in your blood now."

"Yeah."

"Will you talk to Dr. Spinney?"

He nodded. "He thinks I should have therapy with him for a while. I guess it's a good idea."

"Yes, I think it is." She got up, leaving her sandwich untouched, and went over to the balcony wall, leaned against it, looking out.

"I'd like to see you," he said. "When I come into Boston each week to see Dr. Spinney, I'd also like to come here."

"Oh, I'd hate it."

He looked away from her, then heard her laughter.

"You are such an innocent," she said. "I'm teasing you. I'll be hurt if you don't come to see me. I'll be furious with you." She put out her arms toward him. "Come here, will you?"

He joined her at the balcony wall. She was still laughing, shaking her head. "A real gullible innocent," she said. "They're hard to find these days."

"Are they?"

"Yes, but don't change that part of you. It's the best part of all."

Below them the streets were empty and the night city slept through its brief quiet hours. At the corner a traffic light flashed signals for an empty intersection: green, amber, red, green, amber, red, green. . . .